ALMOST A
TURKISH SOAP OPERA

Why do you shame your family?

ADAPTED INTO AN AWARD WINNING FEATURE FILM

Anne-Rae Vasquez

AR Publishing Inc.

This is a work of fiction. The events and characters described here are purely fictional and in no way represent or resemble real life events, places or people.

Cover graphic design by Gabriel Lascu
Edited by Dwayne Edmonson

Amazon 2nd Edition
ISBN 978-0986492105

For Joseph whose stories inspired me to write this book.   And for Adel and his wife, the corner stone of their family.

A big thank you to my producer, cast, crew, family and friends for helping turn this book into an award winning feature film.

Watch the movie at <u>almostaturkishsoapopera.com</u>

Preface

I blame my interest in Turkish soap operas (also known as Turkish TV series) on a sweet Arabic couple from the Middle East. They were my guests for two months and during their stay, the wife said that she missed watching her favourite Arabic-dubbed Turkish soap operas and it made her very homesick. I searched online and found streaming videos of the soap operas. This started a nightly ritual of watching back to back episodes of different series of Turkish soaps. Our marathon watching weekends were full of fun, laughter and drama. We had so many great conversations as we analyzed the characters and the scenes together. I recall the husband telling me that he had no interest in soap operas. However, when it came time to watch the shows, he was always the one who could repeat word for word scenes from past episodes as he critiqued the current storyline.

So welcome and hope you enjoy the story.

PART ONE

Away From Home

Chapter 1

Istanbul, Turkey

The story unfolds on an ordinary day in Adel's life. It was his twenty-fifth birthday and his mother and sisters had given him a simple celebration—making plates of baklava which they spent all morning preparing. His brothers and his friend Kamil bought him a T-shirt that said in English "Looking for wife". It had become a question his mother would repeat over and over—Why hasn't Adel found a bride yet?

His father, a dark skinned, stern looking man, arrives home from a hard day's work in the construction field, still dressed in his muddy work clothes. He sits on the couch, picks up the remote to change the channel to watch what is left of the football game. He lights up a cigarette and sits back enjoying the first few moments of relaxation.

Adel's mother, a light skinned, plump, petite woman, is in the kitchen ironing clothes. Her hair is wrapped in a golden coloured *hijab*, a head scarf worn by religious Muslim women. The hijab frames her face, emphasizing her piercing blue eyes. She is dressed in a traditional long sleeved tunic, the shade of fresh cocoa, which flows down to her feet. Seeing that the ashtray on the coffee table is overflowing with cigarette butts, she bustles in from the kitchen and swiftly replaces the ashtray with a clean one. Without missing a beat, she hurries back into the kitchen, empties the ashtray into the rubbish bin and then tosses it into the sink. She quickly washes her hands with soap and water and dries them on her apron. She returns to her ironing board where she continues ironing the wrinkles out of her sons' jeans and underwear. All the while, her eyes are glued onto the twenty inch television set on the kitchen counter which is playing *"Fatmagülün Suçu Ne (What is*

Fatmagul's Fault?)", one of her many favourite Turkish soap operas.

Adel and his two younger sisters, Juliana and Keananna, sixteen and thirteen years of age, look like carbon copies of each other. All three have the same golden wavy honey blonde hair and emerald green eyes which are uncommon traits to see in people from their local area. Other Turkish people who meet them for the first time are fascinated by their features. Some are intrigued by their unique appearance but most are simply envious of their looks, gossiping about them behind their backs. His baby sister Zeinab has his father's colouring. Her soft skin is the colour of creamy mocha and her baby curls are oil slick black.

Juliana and Keananna are at the kitchen table feeding their baby sister a bowl of warm rice cereal. Like their mother, their attention is also focused on the television set. They noisily explain to their mother the details of what happened in the scene that she just missed. Their mother shushes them quiet. Her look of concentration sends the older girls into a bout of giggles. Zeinab laughs as well, smacking her chubby hands into her cereal.

Meanwhile, Sammy and Jowdat, his two younger brothers, are doing their homework in the enclosed verandah which also serves as the bedroom which all the boys share. Physically they resemble their father but their personalities are their own. Sammy, twenty-two, is laid back and easy going. He idolizes Adel and wants to be just like him. He is very popular at school and has many young girl admirers. Jowdat, seventeen years old, is shy and naïve, always seeing things in a positive light. Like many boys his age, Jowdat has already resigned himself to follow in his father's footsteps and work in construction or in a factory after he finishes high school.

Seeing the opportunity to speak to his father in private, Adel approaches him. He does this cautiously, knowing that he is usually in a sour mood after coming home from work.

"Father, have you spoken to Grand Uncle about what I asked? Will he sign over one of the parcels of your land so that I can build my house on it?" Adel asks.

Adel's father, grumbling under his breath, gets up and walks outside onto the balcony. Adel follows him.

"I am twenty-five years old now. All my cousins were twenty years old when they built their houses and have married and have children since then."

His father shakes his head. "Enough! My head hurts from all this talk!" he yells. He waves him away, refusing to discuss the matter any further.

Infuriated, Adel turns around and marches into his bedroom. His brothers are hunched over the books on their beds. Sammy turns to watch Adel reach for something under his bed. He brings out a small wooden box. He opens the box and pulls out an envelope which contains an airline ticket to Los Angeles, California. Adel has been dreaming about buying an airplane ticket to the USA since he was a child.

Adel sits on his bed, gently placing the box beside him. Sammy tries to see what is in his hand. Adel shifts his shoulder to block his view.

It is time to get his plan into action. Adel pulls out his cell phone and calls his best friend Kamil. Kamil, also twenty-five years old, is dark haired and olive skinned. His thick eyebrows stretch over his large ebony eyes. Unlike Adel's family who is considered upper middle class, Kamil comes from a lower class family. His father works as a private chauffeur for Adel's Grand Uncle. Adel has known Kamil practically since birth.

Kamil asks, "So we really are going to do this?"

"Yes we are leaving like we planned. There is nothing here for me. My father won't do anything to get my Grand Uncle to give him his share of my grandfather's inheritance which means that I will never see my share of the inheritance," Adel says.

"Well, you knew this since we were children. So let's talk about the plan," Kamil says. "Finally, after three years of hard construction work, we have our dream tickets to the land of opportunity and beautiful ladies!" He laughs.

Adel smiles broadly. "Hollywood here we come!"

* * *

Later that night at the dinner table, Adel waits for his family to sit. His brothers and sisters are chattering happily about their day's events. His father sits down last. He frowns as he eats his meal. The thoughts in his head cloud his mind. His mother is busy serving everyone her delicious *köfte*, a popular Middle Eastern dish made of minced lamb or beef meatballs, onto their plates. Adel, unsure when would be the best time to announce the news, decides it is now or never.

"Pa, Ma, I have something to tell you," Adel begins. He coughs into his hand. Adel's father looks up and puts down his fork. He is annoyed that yet again his meal is being interrupted. Is having peace and quiet in his house too much to ask for? Adel's mother smiles. She is eager to hear what her favourite son has to say. His brothers and sisters look at him curiously.

Adel stammers, "I, I, uh... Kamil and I...we are..."

"What Adel? What?" Juliana asks.

"Kamil and I are flying to the United States tomorrow," Adel finally blurts out.

"For holiday? For how long?" Jowdat asks.

Adel takes a deep breath and continues. "We are going to live there for a few months. If it goes well, maybe stay there."

His mother breaks down in tears. She is horrified at the news that her oldest son is leaving home before marriage. His brother and sisters chatter amongst themselves excited for his upcoming adventure.

His father, however, stands up and angrily shouts obscenities, cursing the day this ungrateful son was born. "Who gave you the permission to do this? You chose your path now. Get out of my face!" He slams his fist on the table and leaves.

His mother, still crying, follows her husband while the rest of the family sits awkwardly in silence. Adel excuses himself from the table and goes to his room.

Chapter 2

Hollywood, here we come
Los Angeles, California

One week later, Adel and Kamil arrive at the LAX airport in Los Angeles, California, ready for exciting opportunities. With only their passports, very basic knowledge of English and five thousand US dollars in their wallets split between both of them, they are ready to fulfill their destinies. After passing through US customs, they find their way to the luggage terminal to collect their bags. They ask an airport worker how to get to Hollywood. He points towards a shuttle van parked outside the airport. Not sure of what to do next, Adel decides that they should find a place to stay. They board the shuttle van and start their journey to Hollywood.

The shuttle van drops them off at Hollywood Boulevard and Las Palmas Avenue. Adel and Kamil stand on the corner and are surprised at what they see. It is not exactly how they pictured it would be. Where were all the movie stars, the expensive cars and warm friendly Americans to welcome them into this wonderful city?

Later on in the day, Adel and Kamil wander from hotel to hotel and then to motel. They enquire about what the cost is to spend the night. They soon realize that even the lowest standard motel (where cockroaches and rats infest the walls) costs a minimum of sixty dollars a night. Sixty dollars a night can rent a decent three star hotel room in Istanbul. While walking down Hollywood Boulevard, scantily dressed women approach Adel asking if he and his friend want to have some fun. Adel and Kamil are familiar with what these type of women want. They have seen many of them in certain red area districts in Istanbul.

Finally Adel decides to book a room at a motel on Highland Avenue. It is small and dingy but they are too tired to complain.

After settling in, Adel tells Kamil that he is confident that Hollywood had more in store for them. Kamil, however, is not so sure.

Determined to look his best, Adel attempts to iron his jeans. This would be a first for him since his mother took care of this chore back home. Kamil can't resist giving him advice on how to hold the jean hem just as his own mother would do it. Adel does a terrible job of things. The two bicker back and forth. Kamil teases him saying that he should have packed his mother in his luggage because it looks like he is incapable of taking care of himself. Exasperated by the whole ordeal, Adel throws his jeans on the bed.

Kamil walks over and picks up the jeans. He places them back on the ironing board. In four strokes, he irons out the wrinkles perfectly. He hands them back to Adel whose mouth drops open in amazement. A few seconds later, he and Kamil break out into laughter. It has been a long day. They both decide to postpone their sightseeing for the next morning.

* * *

The next day, Adel and Kamil's first destination is the Beverly Hills shopping mall. They are awed by the splendor of the stores and all the pretty people rushing through. Kamil eyes a pair of four hundred dollar Dolce & Gabbana sunglasses imagining himself wearing them. Adel has his eyes on a Gucci watch, a fancy suit and a pair of genuine cowboy boots. Back home, the cost of all these items put together could feed a family of eight for 6 months.

Kamil tells Adel that all this window shopping is making him very hungry. Your wish is my command, Adel replies.

They savor their first quarter pounder with cheese and a side of large fries at a nearby McDonald's restaurant. A man dressed up in a Ronald McDonald suit invites himself to their table. Out of politeness, Adel motions for him to sit but soon regrets it. The man tells them in a loud voice how lucky they are to be in America, the land of the free. People sitting near their table roll their eyes and mutter comments to themselves. On top of this, his breath smells like sour vinegar and he belches in Adel's face after every sentence as if to stress his point. Finally, Adel politely tells him in broken English that they must hurry to meet their father and it was nice to meet him. The sentence comes out as "We must hurry for the Father of Might will smite you."

Stunned by his words, the man wanders over to another table.

* * *

After a few days, reality begins to sink in. Adel counts the money left in his wallet. His stomach turns into a knot. He calculates that it will only be days before their money runs out.

"Kamil, we are running out of money," Adel says. "Motel rent is seventy-five dollars a night and food is costing us sixty dollars a day."

"The five thousand US dollars we brought isn't going to last very long." Kamil shakes his head.

"We need to find jobs and somewhere we can stay for much less than what we are paying for here at this motel," Adel says.

"I will call Mirwan, my cousin, as we planned. He is the one who lives in Los Angeles and owns his own business." Kamil opens his address book to look for Mirwan's number.

"Yes, the one who runs a shuttle van business that my Grand-Uncle owns. He knows we are here, right?" Adel's mood suddenly picks up.

"Yes, of course. I called him last month and he said to contact him when we arrive in Los Angeles."

"Okay, let's go see him tomorrow." Adel pats Kamil on the back and smiles. He is certain that God will take good care of them.

Chapter 3

Vacation is over

Mirwan shows Adel and Kamil around the shuttle van parking lot. He lets them look at two white older style shuttle vans. Although he is in his early thirties, Mirwan's worn face makes him look much older. Mirwan is dark skinned, short and has a stocky build. Over his large dark eyes sits a bushy untamed "unibrow" and over his lip is a matching moustache. Although he owns the business, Adel notices that Mirwan's drivers dress better than he does. Mirwan looks like he has not washed his worn out golf shirt and faded black pants in weeks. He whispers to Kamil that if he were the boss, he'd be wearing a jacket and a tie. Kamil rolls his eyes and motions for him to lower his voice.

Later in his office, Mirwan gives them a key to his one bedroom apartment. He offers them free room and board as long as they work for him. Mirwan will pay them cash under the table. He makes a few phone calls. In a few days he provides them with fake social security numbers and drivers' licenses.

* * *

After a few weeks, Adel has successfully memorized all the shuttle routes and has learned how to navigate around Los Angeles and the surrounding towns. He is proud of all the cash his tips bring in and wishes he could work twenty four hours straight so he could make more money. On top of this, he actually enjoys driving his customers. He chats with them all the way to their destinations. Although, he speaks in broken English, he picks up the local slang words very quickly. His customers find him charming and like the funny way he pronounces words.

Kamil, on the other hand, finds it difficult to adjust to the job. Although his English speaking is better than Adel's, he is shy and does not talk to his customers unless it is absolutely necessary. He does not bring home half the tips that Adel does. By the end of his shift he feels so drained. He wishes that he doesn't have to go to work the next day.

Mirwan pays their salaries once a week. Adel saves every penny he can. He had asked Mirwan what it would take for him to become an owner-operator. At the time, Mirwan laughed in his face. He told Adel that if he gave him two thousand dollars, he would give him the shuttle van he was driving. He would also agree for Adel to get his own customers provided that he gives Mirwan a twenty percent cut.

Six weeks later, Adel walks into Mirwan's office and hands him two thousand dollars—all in small bills collected from the tips he was saving. Mirwan is dumbfounded. He could not go back on his word and so he reluctantly signs the papers to give Adel ownership of the vehicle.

* * *

Now that Adel is his own boss, he pushes himself to work beyond the normal eight hour shifts. He picks up a skill analyzing people and their personalities based on how they dress and what they are carrying. With this new found expertise, he raises and lowers his rates depending on who the customer is. For instance, for a trip from the airport to Long Beach for a group of five well-dressed Japanese tourists carrying fancy electronic gadgets, such as cell phones and cameras, he may charge them a group rate of one hundred and fifty dollars. The regular rate for this trip is twelve dollars per person.

He has observed that the Japanese are too polite to argue with him even if the rate seems unreasonable. Plus, he knows how to slather them with his good looks and charm.

Chapter 4

The shuttle van business

It is a Sunday afternoon and Adel has just finished his shift. Kamil is getting ready to go to work. Adel lies down on his bed—a dirty twin sized mattress on the floor of Mirwan's cluttered one bedroom apartment.

"If it weren't for Mirwan letting us stay at his place and giving us jobs and paying us in cash, I don't know where we'd be right now," Kamil says.

Adel makes a face. "Yeah, don't forget that he's also working us for less than the minimum wage."

"But he managed to get us drivers' licenses and social security cards. The only thing is I still can't figure how to get around LA yet."

"I know all the towns, highways, cities." Adel smiles broadly.

"Hmph. That's because you're working double shifts. You're working so hard," Kamil replies.

"I'm working hard for the tips. Without the tips, I wouldn't have saved enough to buy my own shuttle van. That's how I got Mirwan to get me to be an owner-operator."

"And why would Mirwan agree to that?"

"I have to pay him twenty percent of the profits."

Kamil gasps. "Wow, that's a pretty big cut!"

"Well, if I didn't work eighteen hours a day and also change the shuttle rates, I wouldn't have saved the money so quickly."

"What do you mean change the shuttle rates? We are not allowed to do that. I thought the rates are fixed." Kamil knew this was against the rules. How could Adel do such a thing?

"Well, that's why I only change rates with foreign customers," Adel says.

Kamil feigns interest. "How do you know what rate to give to what customer?"

Adel lowers his voice. "This is how I do it... For the past few weeks, I try this. I look for a group of five Japanese tourists, let's say. They will be playing with their electronic toys like the Nokia cell phones, Sony cameras, and JVC camcorders. You know the ones like we see at Circuit City. So when I get a group like this, I charge them one hundred fifty dollars to go from the airport to Long Beach."

Kamil is surprised. "But that should only be a sixty dollar fare!"

"You are a very good student, Kamil." Adel pats him on the shoulder.

After a few minutes, Kamil brings up the fact that their visitor visas have expired. "Should we ask Mirwan if he can help us get work status visas?"

Adel has never trusted Mirwan but out of politeness he has never said anything aloud since Kamil and Mirwan were cousins. Lately though, he noticed that Mirwan was rude to him, often speaking in a bossy condescending tone. What he didn't know was that Kamil had to beg Mirwan to give Adel a job. Mirwan told him that he didn't like Adel because he was full of himself. Kamil knew that the only reason why Mirwan finally let Adel work for him was because he feared Adel's Grand Uncle.

"No, no... I do not want any more favours from him. I know he's your cousin but to tell you the truth, dude (a new word he learned), I don't trust him," Adel says.

Kamil looks at his watch. "Hey, I have to go do my shift now. I will see you later." He grabs his lunch bag from the kitchen counter and leaves.

Adel finally has the place to himself. He begins counting his cash and putting them in bundles. He places each bundle into small dark plastic grocery bags wrapping them tight. When he is done, he hides the money throughout the apartment in obscure locations—in the ceiling, under a floor board, behind the drywall and on top of the highest cabinets. As a child, he always hid his money all over his home. But it seemed no matter where he hid his money, his father would find it and spend it on cigarettes or gamble it away playing cards with his friends. When he grew older, he learned how to be more creative at hiding his money and soon his father gave up trying to locate his hiding spots.

He always took care of his mother knowing that his father often spent the money for food on his own expenses such as cigarettes or other unnecessary items such as the latest model of cell phones. Even though his mother could hardly manage to put food on the table, his father always had the money to spend to buy the latest cell phone. His father is always the first person in the neighbourhood to put an order for one, once the newest model comes out in the market. The funny thing is he rarely receives any phone calls. He simply enjoys the fact that he is the first person in town to own that particular gadget.

When he was a teenager, what drove his mother crazy was the fact that his father never threw anything away even after the device stopped working. In the attic, his father hid a big box of archaic cell phones, chargers and other devices. About once a year, he would bring down the big box (much to Adel's mother's dismay) and let Adel and his brothers go through his collection. Jowdat, the clown that he was, would impersonate his father. He would pick up the very first cell phone his father ever owned (which looked like a black brick and was just as heavy) and wag his finger into the phone. He would pretend he was talking to the local baker, cursing him for giving stale bread for the price of fresh bread, just as his father had done many times in the past. Adel, Sammy and his sisters would burst out laughing. His father used to laugh along with them—denying that he sounded or looked that ridiculous.

Thoughts of his family make Adel homesick. He decides to   phone his family. He searches Kamil's binder for a long distance calling card. Kamil was always good at keeping such things on hand. He finds four calling cards in the front pocket of the cover and takes two for himself.   He dials his home phone number in Istanbul.

Adel's mother answers the phone. She is excited to hear her son's voice. As always, she fires him off the usual questions. Adel tries to steer the conversation.

"Yes, Ma. I am eating well. Did you get the money I sent to you?"

"Yes my son, I did. Thank you very much. Are you sure you and Kamil don't need this for yourselves?" Adel's mother sounds worried.

"Ma, we are fine. Just promise me to not let Father know that you have this money. Use it to pay the bills and buy groceries and if there is any left, save it for when you need it."

"Oh, Adel. You are such a good son. I miss you so much" She starts to cry. "When are you coming home?"

Adel always hates when his mother is upset. "Ma, I have to go now. Please say hello and send my love to the boys Jowdat and Sammy. Kisses and hugs to the girls, Juliana, Keananna, and Zeinab. Let Father know I am okay and I wish him well. I love you Ma."

Adel's mother is still crying. "Yes, yes, I will do that. Please call us again soon. God be with you my son."

Chapter 5

An unexpected surprise

It is early in the morning and Adel is sitting in his van at the international arrivals area at the LAX airport, waiting for customers to arrive. His goal is to find seven passengers to maximize his profits for one trip. He sees a group of people coming out of the airport looking for a ride. Other shuttle van drivers start walking towards the group calling them to ride with them. Adel is not concerned because he knows who he wants. He spots a group of five Japanese tourists who seem a bit lost. He comes up to them and says in a sweet voice, "Welcome, welcome to Los Angeles. Let me help you with your baggage."

They are somewhat startled. The youngest man in the group quickly types in his electronic translator. He pushes his glasses up with his finger and speaks in broken English, "We go to Disnee rand hotel."

Adel smiles. "No problem, Disney Land hotel. I take you." The group of men appear relieved and they proceed to follow Adel to the van.

The older man of the group shyly asks Adel, "How much?"

"Good price. Fifty percent off for group rate," Adel says. "For all of you, two hundred dollars."

The man smiles and nods his head. He translates to the others happy that Adel is giving them fifty percent off.

Adel is having a good morning and helps them all inside. He looks around to find two more passengers. He spots an older European couple dressed in matching sport clothes, and he says to himself, "This is my day." He starts to approach them when an attractive woman in her early thirties pulling a large duffel bag and a backpack comes towards him blocking his view of his potential clients.

"Excuse me! Shuttle driver! Excuse me… can you please help me with my stuff?"

Adel frowns—can't this girl see that he is busy? He continues walking by her towards the older couple. The woman is now walking behind him calling out, "Please, can you help me with my stuff? I need to get to Anaheim."

He shakes his head. "Sorry miss, I'm not going that way."

She grabs his arm and stops him. "Oh yeah, then why is that guy in your van keep saying, *'Yay, I's going to Deesnee Rand'*, and the sign on your van says Anaheim."

Adel looks back at the van and sure enough, his Japanese passenger is gleefully dancing beside the van, waving at other tourists while singing *"I going to Deesnee Rand."*

Adel looks down at the woman. "I don't know what you are talking about. Now please let me go."

The woman grabs his elbow again. "You know you can lose your license for this. I can report you for discriminating me because I'm a woman!"

Adel snaps. "I'm not discriminating you because you're a woman." He lowers his voice and looks around and says, "I'm discriminating you because you're a local!" and he pulls his arm from her grip.

Unfortunately, the couple he had his eyes on earlier are now being escorted away by another shuttle driver from a rival company.

"Hey!" the woman cries out, "Come on, help me out here. You're going to Anaheim anyway, what's one more person?"

Adel rolls his eyes and turns back to her. "Okay, let's go but it's going to cost you twenty-five dollars."

The woman puts her hand on her hips. "The going rate to Anaheim is seventeen dollars and that's all you're getting. Get it? Got it? Good!" and she turns around and gets inside the passenger side of the van slamming the door shut.

Adel gives a big sigh and shakes his head, picks up her bags and puts them in the back of the van.

After the luggage is loaded and his passengers are ready to go, Adel begins driving to Anaheim. The woman who drove him crazy earlier is seated beside him on the passenger side.

She asks him, "So where are you from?"

Adel replies quickly, "Los Angeles."

She shakes her head. "No really…where are you from originally?"

"Originally? From Hollywood but now Los Angeles," he replies quickly. "Can we stop this interrogation? I need to focus on driving." Although he often asks this same question to his customers, he is uncomfortable when strangers ask him about his own background. Who knows? What if this lady was an undercover immigration officer underneath that charming smile and pretty dress? He shakes his head and tries to focus on the road.

She laughs softly and looks out the window. "Let me guess… East European? Hmm…no…your accent doesn't sound like that…Greek? No…I'd know a Greek accent if I heard it. Definitely Mediterranean…Am I close?"

Adel turns to look at her. "I am surprised with your knowledge of accents. Most American girls I have met thought that Turkey was the capital of Australia." He smiles in spite of himself and says gruffly, "You live in Anaheim?"

The woman smiles. "No, I'm just visiting with my father for the summer. I actually live in British Columbia, Canada."

Adel asks, "Are you Canadian then?"

She nods. "Well, I have dual citizenship. Canadian and American. I've been living in BC and LA back and forth since I was thirteen when my parents got divorced. I prefer Canada though. Cleaner, nicer, safer... that's why I only come down here for a couple of weeks to visit with my dad."

He gives her a glance and notices that she looks mixed, possibly Chinese and American. He notices that her eyes are a deep blue green colour much like his own. The shape of her eyes is almond-like, giving her face an exotic look. He shakes his head and turns back to the road. They continue their conversation as he drives. Slowly, he allows himself to joke with her. He has decided that she seems too nice to be an immigration officer.

The van now arrives at the first stop—the Disneyland Hotel. His Japanese passengers start climbing out. They are chattering in Japanese and snapping photos while waiting for their luggage. Adel unloads their bags and places them on the sidewalk. With his Polaroid camera in hand, the younger Japanese tourist motions to Adel to stand near the other members of his group. He calls out to the woman passenger, "Come heer, Missy, Missy. We want to take picture of you preety lady."

Amused, the woman gets out of the van. The Japanese tourists wave for her to stand beside Adel. He smiles, trying to contain his laughter. She gives him a wink as she walks towards him. He casually places his arm around her. She looks up at him, a little surprised but not annoyed. He smiles at her and points toward the camera, reminding her that they had to get ready for the shot.

The young Japanese tourist points his camera to the group and counts to three in Japanese, "Iche, ne, san… Cheeeeesssee!!!" The camera, an instamatic, flashes and in seconds a photo slides out the front. "Again! Again, pleeze minna. Everybuddy." He points the camera again and everyone freezes their poses for another shot. The young man, pleased with himself, pushes his glasses up with one finger and grabs the photo with his other hand. His friends come around him eager to see the photo. Adel, being much taller than all of them simply bends his head over one of them to see the photo in the young man's hands. The picture's image starts to appear. The group of men chatters excitedly in Japanese, pleased with how the photo has turned out. The woman stands to the side watching the interesting spectacle in front of her. Adel turns around and nods his head at her to come take a look. As she comes towards them, the Japanese tourists politely move aside to let her in. The young man offers the photo to her with both his hands outstretched as if surrendering a peace offering.

The photo displays the group, very happily smiling. But in particular, she notices that Adel and her look very much like a couple – a very happy couple. She smiles and nods her head. "Beautiful, Utsukushii," she says. She hands the photo to Adel. He looks at it and then discretely slips it into his shirt pocket.

The young Japanese tourist now hands Adel the payment for the shuttle service. He turns to speak with the other men in the group. Then he smiles and bows as he hands Adel an additional twenty dollar tip.

"Tip. Tip. Zenk you veddy muchy!"

Adel accepts the tip. "Dōmo arigatō and Sayōnara," he says in Japanese. He learned how to say thank you and good-bye in Japanese because he knows it pleases his customers from the land of the sun. The whole group burst out into laughter impressed with his knowledge of Japanese phrases. They bow and repeat the same phrases back to him. He in turn bows to them again and then turns and waves good-bye.

Adel and the woman are the only passengers left in the van. He starts driving. "So what is address to drop you?" he asks.

She smiles. "You mean, what address do you want to be dropped off at?"

He frowns. "I said that, no?"

She shakes her head and gives him a piece of paper with the address.

"Sorry, I teach English as a second language at the university so I have a bad habit of correcting everyone's grammar. It drives all my friends crazy." She laughs to herself.

He makes a turn down a side street and drives slowly till he finds the address. He stops and parks the car and they both turn to each other – an awkward moment.

"Well...thanks. Here's twenty-five dollars." She hands him the bills.

He shakes his head. "No, seventeen dollars is the charge."

She smiles and pushes the money back to him, "Well, consider the rest a tip." She turns to get out of the van.

He is caught off guard. He takes her bags out from the back and brings them to her. He takes the money from his pocket and hands it to her.

"Here, please take this back."

She is surprised. "No, no... why are you..?"

He pauses and then says, "This trip was the most interesting conversation I have with someone since I come to US. I cannot accept money for it." He gives her a smile—this time it is genuine.

She nods her head slowly. "Well, okay... thank you. But if you won't take my money, then I will take you for coffee. And I won't take no for an answer. Help bring my bags in, please."

He stifles a chuckle as he picks up her bags. "Yes, mademoiselle. As you wish…"

She turns back and smiles. "Nora, Nora Lee Morgan. It is a pleasure to meet you." She stretches out her hand.

"Adel Emre. Pleasure to meet you too." They shake hands.

Chapter 6

Where dreams come from

Adel parks outside the LAX airport. They enjoy watching the planes land and take off on the runways. Earlier they had stopped at Starbucks coffee shop. Nora kept her promise and bought Adel a coffee, even though Adel insisted on paying. Nora offered to buy him an iced cappuccino or mocha, but he politely refused. He was not fond of the fancy flavors or different types of coffee. Black coffee was the closest to Turkish coffee you could get at American coffee shops.

"So you are here in America because you think you can fulfill all your hopes and dreams?" she asks.

He nods his head. "Back in my country, I feel like every day is being in jail. No future, nothing for myself. I wake up every day and go to do the only work available for all men my age... construction. I finish college as an engineer and work hard to graduate. In the end, I work like a dog, like my father who did not finish high school. And if I stay, in a couple years, my mother and father will arrange for me to marry a cousin from the village. "

"Is that such a bad thing?" she asks. "It seems your family works hard to live a good clean decent life. Take my family for instance, both my parents are remarried and have kids with their new spouses. I don't feel close to either of them. I've always had to take care of myself."

He sighs. "You do not understand. All my life, I feel helpless. My father is a good man but he is weak. His father who was head of the family died when my father was a child. His Uncle, my Grand Uncle, became head and from that day on, he treat my dad like he is nobody. To this day, my father's inheritance has not been given to him. Grand Uncle always saying he has to wait because of one reason or another. But then my family live like very poor people while my Grand Uncle and his children and children's children are living like kings and queens."

She nods her head. "I see."

He continues. "At my age being the oldest, I should have already my own land to build my house so that I can prepare for marriage. But no, my cousins all have their land and houses while my father does nothing to fight for what is rightfully ours. I see my mother working so hard to feed all eight of us while my father brings home his pay cheque is not enough for a family of three. We live in a two bedroom suite in the first floor of my Grand Uncle's house."

He shakes his head. Just thinking about it makes him angry. "His married daughters live on their own floors above us with my Grand Uncle and his wife on the top floor. And then there are three new houses beside us where his sons and sons of his sons live. We live with my father's side of the family but they treat us as strangers. We do not play with them and they do not see us."

Nora frowns. "That sounds very strange. You live all together on the same property. You would think that your family would be much closer."

Adel shrugs. "They do not talk to my mother. My mother who is the kindest nicest woman in the world but they treat her like she is not existing." Adel struggles to find the English words to explain. "And my father... what does he do? Absolutely nothing. Just smokes and smokes in front of the TV set watching his football and news while the world passes us by."

She nods her head. "So are you the one who keeps the family together? You help your mom with your brothers and sisters, I am guessing..."

He nods. "Yes, and I always have part time job when I was school age and I always give my mother money to help out. Even now, I send money home to her because it is my family and I need to help them."

Nora is amazed. "Gosh, guys here only care about themselves. I doubt if any of them would send money home to their parents. Half of them are still living at home, unemployed, lazy moochers."

He frowns. "Moochers?"

She laughs. "Like a leech. They just keep taking and taking without giving anything in return."

He nods. "Ahhh... I see." He wonders why he has told this perfect stranger so much about his life. He has never lowered his guard to anyone much less someone he had just known for a few hours. He trusted her and she seemed honestly interested in learning more about him. They continue talking as the planes take off and land in the distance. Overall, it has been an interesting day.

Later in the evening, Adel drives Nora to her father's home. He helps her out of the van and brings her bags to the door.

"Well, good night and thank you." She smiles. She stretches out her hand to him.

He grasps her hand with both of his. "Can we do this again sometime? I really enjoyed this evening."

She nods her head, smiling. "Yes, I would love that." She pulls out a pen and a scrap piece of paper from her purse and writes down her phone and puts it in his pocket. Moved by the moment, he touches her cheek and they kiss... a sweet long kiss. Her heart is beating hard and she wonders if he can hear it. All he is thinking is how velvety her lips feel against his.

After what seems an eternity, they finally pull away, smiling dreamily at each other. She puts her keys in the door. Before opening the door, she turns back to him. Adel stares, her silhouette under the porch light is surreal. She waves and blows him a kiss. He smiles and waves back at her.

Then he turns and gets back into the van. He puts the keys into the ignition. Before he starts the engine, he pulls out the photo from his pocket and looks at it. Smiling back at him is the group of Japanese tourists. He focuses his attention on the image of himself with his arm wrapped around Nora. He folds the picture so that only he and Nora are visible. He slips the photo into his wallet.

The radio crackles with the dispatcher's voice filling the van. He needs to get back to work. He quickly puts the photo back into his pocket, turns the engine on and drives away.

Chapter 7

Mirwan

Mirwan and Adel are getting ready to leave for work. Adel is whistling and humming. Mirwan glares at him. How can this FOB, this *fresh off the boat*, bum come here with absolutely nothing and then be able to make his business a success in only a few months?

As for himself, just immigrating to America from Istanbul was a feat. He, like most of his family, was employed by Adel's Grand Uncle. Although technically, Adel's Grand Uncle wasn't related to Mirwan, he and everyone he knew also addressed him as Grand Uncle out of respect. He was a rich and powerful man and was known in their hometown as the Izmir Grand Uncle (which is almost like the Sicilian Godfather).

During his teens, Mirwan had the honour of being the Grand Uncle's errand boy. Unknown to his family though, he was really employed to do the Grand Uncle's dirty work.

In his early twenties, when he decided to move to Los Angeles, the Grand Uncle helped finance the trip and his accommodations. But like most things, nothing comes for free. The Grand Uncle made sure that he knew that he still was the boss. He struggled to establish his shuttle business for many years. The Grand Uncle helped him financially by assigning him to do special "jobs" in America for him.

His latest assignment is to take care of Adel and make sure to report everything about him back to Istanbul. So now one of his top priorities is babysitting Adel, the Grand Uncle's golden boy. If it were up to him, he would have left Adel on the street.

Adel stands in front of the mirror in the living room to comb his hair. He straightens his tie and his shirt. The sight of him makes Mirwan's eyes burn. Who does he think he is? Adel pulls out some money from his wallet and counts it in front of him, still humming to himself. Kamil patiently waits for Adel on the couch.

Mirwan says in a sarcastic tone, "Better not spend it all in one place, Adel. You never know when your luck might run out."

Although Adel can't stand Mirwan, he is in too good of a mood to let him get under his skin. "I think you deserve a new shirt. You have been wearing the same three shirts since we come here to LA." He hands Mirwan a twenty dollar bill.

Mirwan makes a face. "You came here with nothing and now you think you are somebody."

Adel flashes him a disarming smile. "That's where you're wrong, my friend. I was somebody *before* I came here." He turns to the mirror again and runs his fingers through his hair one last time.

Mirwan gives him a look of disgust, turns around and walks out of the apartment, slamming the door behind him.

Adel shakes his head and gives Kamil a look. He really needs to discuss with him about finding a new place to move into. But for now, he had another goal. He counts out one thousand US dollars.

Adel brags, "Don't worry Kamil. I can make this thousand dollars easy in one day of work."

Kamil is not convinced. "Are you sure, Adel? Shouldn't we save this in case we need it in the future?"

Adel is not concerned. "Let's enjoy what our hard work has brought us. Come on, I know you were looking at the D&G sunglasses when we were at Beverly Hills Shopping mall."

Kamil shakes his head but pleased that Adel remembered. "No, no... that is much too expensive. They cost four hundred dollars. You can't possibly spend that kind of money for sunglasses."

Adel laughs. "Come on, Kamil... You worry too much. But I understand. I know you won't sleep at night if you owned sunglasses that cost more than your car back home. We'll get you ones that are really good knock-offs." Adel's excitement has now rubbed off on Kamil. He grabs his jacket. "Come on, let's go."

At the Beverly Hills shopping mall, Adel and Kamil are here not to window shop but with a mission to spend some big bucks. The first stop is the Gucci store. Ten minutes later, Adel is sporting a new Gucci watch on his wrist. Other shoppers are smiling at him, his happiness so infectious.

Adel proudly shows off his new watch to Kamil.

"Come on, Kamil. Ask me what time is it."

Kamil cannot stop himself from saying, "Three hundred dollars for a watch? That could feed a whole village for a month in Istanbul. Really, it could."

Adel laughs and punches him on the arm. He runs ahead towards another store.

When Kamil catches up to him, he sees Adel trying on a suit that reminds him of what he sees pimps in Hollywood wear. Adel looks pleased at what he sees as he admires himself in the mirror. Kamil peeks at the price tag. Three hundred dollars. Now why would that shock him?

Dressed in his new pimp suit, Adel walks through the mall. He hears 50 Cent's *P.I.M.P* rap song in his head as he struts past each store. His eyes light up when he sees something in the display window of a men's shoe store. He walks inside and beelines straight to the counter. A short soft spoken shoe salesman comes out to greet him. He eyes Adel up and down and compliments him on his attire.

Adel smiles broadly. "Bring me the cowboy boots that I see in your display window in size European 43, young man." The salesman nods. He hurries to the back of the store to find the boots.

Meanwhile, Kamil wanders around looking at the different styles of shoes. He hears the salesman return. He sees him holding shiny brown snakeskin cowboy boots. Oh my goodness!

"Just like Clint Eastwood." Adel says to Kamil.

Kamil looks at the price on the box. "But they cost two hundred fifty dollars!"

"Well, it is a good deal. This gentleman here says it is made of real African snake skin." The salesman smiles shyly. Kamil shakes his head watching Adel as he struts around him in his new cowboy boots.

Chapter 8

All going so well

Adel sits in his shuttle van admiring his new dark tan brief case. He spins the gold combination lock and caresses the leather. Adel remembers when he was six years old. He would sit by the stairs outside his home watching as his Grand Uncle came home from work carrying a briefcase just like the one he now owned. Adel used to look longingly at the briefcase wondering what important papers were inside. A man with a briefcase was a man who was worth something.

He suddenly remembered standing in the same spot by the stairs and seeing his father returning home from work. A truck would pull up outside with all the workers piled in the back. His father would wave goodbye to his coworkers and then come up to the house. He would be filthy from working on a construction job site all day. In his hand he would carry a worn cloth bag used to carry his lunch. Adel remembers feeling embarrassed as he watched his father remove his shoes and dust his feet in the doorway of their home. How can he ever be proud of his father? What has he accomplished? He vowed to himself that he will never be like his father. He will achieve more than what his status in life has to offer him.

In the apartment, Adel and Kamil are getting ready for work. Adel reaches for his brief case and he notices that it is unlocked. Mirwan's face comes into his mind and he pictures him sifting through his papers. His face hardens. "Mirwan, that dog!"

Kamil looks up. "What?"

Adel turns around. "Kamil, we have to find our own place." His face is red with anger.

Kamil takes a deep breath. He has been dreading having to tell his good friend of his own news. "No, I want to tell you before but..." He pauses.

Adel interrupts. "But what?"

Kamil continues. "I am going to Canada at the end of the month."

Adel is stunned. "What? Why Kamil? We are doing so well here."

Kamil can't believe Adel's ignorance. He shakes his head. "No, you are doing well. I am not. I hate driving the van. This life is not for me." He gathers his keys and wallet from his drawer. "I have family in Vancouver, Canada. They have a friend who has a daughter who they want to arrange for us to be married." He stops to look at Adel who is speechless. "I do not see a future here."

Adel slowly nods his head as the information sinks in. "It's okay, Kamil. I understand. You're my best friend. I just can't believe you are leaving." He comes over to Kamil. "You are like a brother to me. If you are happy, then that is all that matters." He gives him a hug.

Kamil's eyes lighten up. "You can come with me. We can take the English program at the university together. I really think there is no future here in LA for me and for you."

Adel shakes his head. "No, I will stay. I have my business now and I cannot just leave it to go to Canada."

Kamil's smile leaves his face. "I know you will say this. If you change your mind later, my home is your home." They have always done things together since they were children. Adel could not imagine not having him around. Although he is disappointed, he smiles and hugs his good friend again.

Chapter 9

Shut up, Ahab

It has been a few days since Kamil has left for Canada. It felt so strange to not have him nearby. Since he was a child, he couldn't remember when he was not a phone call away.

Adel is parked in his usual spot outside the airport. He thought about Nora many times. He almost called her number but he wasn't in the mood to go on a date.

Suddenly there is a knock on his window. Startled, he looks up to see two uniformed men standing outside his door.

The larger of the two is massive, probably an ex-marine, with blond hair cropped in a military style crew cut and the build of a sumo wrestler.

"Get out of the car now with your hands up!"

"What did I do wrong, Officer?" Adel asks calmly.

The shorter officer reminds him of Eric Estrada, his favourite American actor from the TV series called "C.H.i.P.s". Older American TV series such as C.H.i.P.s, Knight Rider, were very popular to watch when he was a child growing up in Istanbul.

Officer Estrada yells at him. "Shut up. You are coming with us." He opens his door and both officers flash their badges at him.

"Was I parked illegally?" Adel asks, trying to make sense of it all.

The larger officer smirks. "I.C.E. We're from U.S. Immigration and Customs Enforcement. You are under arrest for working and residing in the United States illegally."

They shove him into the side of the van and handcuff him. Passersby stop and stare at the commotion the officers are causing. Other shuttle van drivers who he considered friends whisper to each other when they recognize Adel. The two I.C.E. officers drag Adel to their car and push him inside and lock the door. More I.C.E. officers surround his van and start searching through it. The officer resembling Eric Estrada climbs inside the vehicle.

"Where are you taking me? What's going to happen to my van?" Adel asks.

The officer looks back at him disgustedly. "Shut up, Ahab. We ask the questions around here." He starts the car and begins to drive.

Adel watches helplessly as they drive past his shuttle van. One I.C.E. officer is carrying out his briefcase from the van. Another is going through the back of the van.

He had imagined this scene in his head a hundred times when he first started his shuttle business but over the months, he had grown complacent convinced that he and Kamil would never be caught. *What is going to happen to me now?*

Chapter 10

Detained, dejected and disillusioned

Adel sits on the bottom of a bunk bed in the immigration detention center. The orange prison jumpsuit feels rough against his skin. Beside him in the other bunk is an older man named Moe who is originally from Iran. Moe tells him that he has been in the detention for years.

Not knowing who to turn to, Adel makes a phone call to Mirwan for help. Mirwan tells him that he spoke with an immigration lawyer. The lawyer told him that Adel can try to appeal and perhaps claim asylum but since Turkey is considered an ally of the US, the chances of winning are slim. The other option is for Adel to ask to be deported back to Turkey. Otherwise, he will have to stay locked up indefinitely.

Moe tells him about others that have been there for years waiting to appeal. He reveals to Adel how living in the USA was not a rosy haven for most of the illegal aliens. Many had resorted to working as slave labourers.

"I have been here for fifteen years and Chun has been here for ten." He nods towards a short skinny Asian man playing cards with four other men. "Others have been here for five years or less."

Adel can't comprehend anyone wanting to stay for years in this place. "Why would you stay so long here?"

"I have no choice. If I go back to my country, I would be tried for my political beliefs and then sentenced to death," Moe says in a matter of fact tone.

Adel's eyes widen. "That is awful."

"If I could go back home, I would. I miss my family and my friends. Are you also running from your country?" Moe asks.

"No... not at all. I have no worries about going back home to Turkey." Adel's only worry was facing his friends and family. It would be so humiliating to return so shamefully. But losing your pride and losing your life were two completely different things to face. He would rush home in a heartbeat if that were his only choice.

Moe says quietly, "Then the answer for you is simple."

Adel nods his head slowly. "Yes, it is simple."

Chapter 11

Deportation

A few weeks later, Adel is standing in front of the judge in a small court room. He had been waiting for hours outside in the holding cell with others like himself. He had met the lawyer Mirwan hired for only for a few minutes before seeing the judge. It was so confusing and chaotic that he wasn't sure what the outcome would be.

The judge removes his glasses and looks at Adel up and down. Finally, he clears his throat. "Well, you really do not look like you belong here. I think the best option for you is to return to Turkey."

Adel bites his lip and looks at the lawyer who whispers to him. "This is the best thing for you to do. Otherwise you could be waiting here for years with the same conclusion in the end."

Adel cannot see himself losing years of his life in this hell hole. Moe had given him the best advice.

He tells the judge, "Please Your Honour. Send me home as soon as possible."

The judge nods his head and hits the gavel on the stone. "You will be deported to Turkey tomorrow. And my advice is to make sure that if you decide to return to the United States, you better have your paperwork in order. The next time will not be so easy."

The next day Adel walks through the LAX airport. The immigration officers have him handcuffed and dragged like a sheep to the slaughter house. Having been stationed at the LAX airport for the past six months, he had come to know a lot of airport staff. Some of them he even called his friends. But today he had no friends. The airport personnel, other shuttle drivers and the travelers stare at him as if he were a criminal. This does not crush Adel's will. He walks with his head held high. He had done nothing wrong. He was only trying to survive.

When they come closer to the gate, a young family who is standing at the counter let Adel and the immigration officer step ahead of them in the line-up. The father grabs his children close to him. His wife, in a low voice, tells him to move back to their seats.

Adel stares at the airplanes outside the window. The immigration officer chats with the pretty blonde stewardess at the counter. When the paperwork is taken care of, both officers escort him onto the plane. On the plane, Officer Estrada leads him to his seat. Everyone on the plane stares at him. When he is seated, the immigration officer removes the handcuffs.

He says, "Now you be a good Ahab and don't cause me any grief."

Adel turns and looks out the window. He pictures Kamil when they first flew to the USA. Kamil could not contain his excitement. He loved having the beautiful stewardesses waiting on him. He was constantly pressing the call button to ask them to bring him more bags of nuts or cans of cola. No matter how annoying he was becoming, the stewardesses always came with a pleasant smile on their face. He used the opportunity to charm them with jokes when they came by. By the end of the trip, at least two of them had scribbled their phone numbers on a cocktail napkin. Kamil kept the napkin as a souvenir.

Today the flight is nothing like the first time. He sits in silence for most of the flight. His thoughts race as he tries to think of the events that had happened in the last year. Halfway through the flight, when the officer finally falls asleep, Adel pulls out the Polaroid picture of himself and Nora from his wallet. In the picture, his arm is draped around Nora's shoulder. Her face is beaming, her smile lighting up the picture. He can smell her perfume as he closes his eyes. He can hear her sweet voice in his ear. These are the thoughts that finally help Adel fall into a deep sleep.

After many hours in the air, the plane lands in Istanbul, Turkey. The immigration officer snaps the handcuffs back on him as they wait for everyone to leave the plane. He feels numb and cannot wait to go home and have a bath.

When they walk off the airplane, there is a tall, large Turkish immigration officer with a bushy moustache waiting for them at the bottom of the stairs. The shorter officer marches up to the Turkish officer. He turns to Adel and snaps, "Stay right there, Ahab."

The Turkish immigration officer tells the American officer to hand over Adel's passport. The officer hesitates before giving the passport to him.

The Turkish officer looks at the passport. "Remove his handcuffs!" After which, he hands Adel his passport, shakes his hand and says in English so that the American immigration officer can hear, "Welcome back home, son." Adel takes his passport and puts it in his pocket. He thanks the Turkish officer in Turkish and turns and walks onto the tarmac. He is back on his Turkish soil—his homeland. His thoughts and emotions are racing in his mind. As he walks by the American immigration officer (giving him the middle finger), the only thought ringing in his head is—*How am I going to get back to Los Angeles?*

Chapter 12

Homeward bound

Adel is back home in Istanbul. His mother and brothers and sisters are bustling around very happy to have him home. In the background, he can hear the TV set playing a Turkish soap opera. Everything here seems to have stood still in time. His head is spinning. His mother tells him about how his father had not been paid for the past month. Many people at his job have been laid off. She and her sisters are trying to prepare healthy meals for the family but they are running low on the basic staple foods. She says even his father has not smoked as much as he used to. He gathers the cigarette butts and puffs on them when he craves to smoke more.

Later, she prepares for him a bowl of lentil soup and he eats it like a man who has been starved for days. He doesn't feel like socializing with his family right now. He decides to get cleaned up. He goes into the bathroom to have a shower. He stares at himself in the mirror. He has not shaven in days and his face is covered with a light beard. His eyes are red and his hair is long and greasy. He washes his face and then starts to shave. He can hear his brothers and sisters whispering outside the door.

Zenaib, his youngest sister, is now speaking in sentences. She knocks on the door and cries out, "Adel, big brother. Come carry me. I miss you!"

He misses her too, he tells her through the door. He smiles as he shaves off the last bit of hair on his chin. He goes into the shower stall and takes a long hot shower. The water soothes his sore muscles and relaxes his thoughts. What is he going to say to his father when he gets home? Probably nothing. What is there to say?

Late in the afternoon, his father comes home from work dressed in the same clothes he wore the day Adel left for America. His father is shocked to see him. Apparently his mother wanted it to be a surprise. *Thanks, Ma.* They both stare at each other for some time before Adel's father walks by him to his room. Adel's mother comes around and gives Adel a reassuring pat on the shoulder. It has only been ten hours since he arrived from the airport and already he feels suffocated.

He gets up and brings the phone to his old room. In his room, Adel is holding his address book. He dials Kamil's phone number in Canada. A woman answers the phone in English.

Adel says, "Hello, please I want to speak to Kamil." He hears the woman yell, "Kamil! Phone call for you!" There is some rustling and hushed conversation between Kamil and his wife on the phone. Adel waits and then he hears Kamil's familiar voice.

"Hello?"

"Kamil, it's me."

Kamil's voice lightens up. "Adel! How are you? How is LA?"

Adel pauses. "I am home in Istanbul."

Kamil sounds puzzled. "Visiting the family?"

Adel sighs. "No, I was arrested last month and was in the detention for the past thirty days. Finally I got to see the judge who told me that there was no reason for me to be there if I did not want to apply for asylum. I was deported yesterday."

Kamil is silent for a few seconds. "Wow, why would you be arrested? How would anyone know you are in the US illegally?"

Adel nods his head slowly. "Yes, I have been thinking this for the past few weeks. The only ones who know is you and Mirwan. The officers were waiting for me at the airport and they got me when I was inside my shuttle van. They knew when I would be there I think. So Kamil, I ask you... do you think Mirwan would do such a thing?"

Kamil pauses to think and then says, "You know Adel...anything is possible. I hate to think my cousin would do this. It is a disgusting thing for him to do this to you."

"I want to go back," Adel says. "My business is there. My van, my things, my money is in Mirwan's place."

Kamil is shocked. "Why risk going back? The US immigration might arrest you again and you will go to the detention. I do not think that the judge will be easier on you the second time. And if Mirwan is behind this, he might have taken all your things already."

Adel can't believe what he is hearing. "He won't know about the money I hid. And I need my van. This is not fair!"

Kamil softens his tone. "Adel, I understand. But the risk is too high. It's not worth it. Why not come to Canada? It is very beautiful here, the people are nicer. You can stay with my wife and me and her family, until you find a place. Come here and study English with me. The university has a great atmosphere and you can meet lots of people. At least come for vacation and decide later if you want to stay."

Adel thinks for a moment. "Kamil, you may have a point. Canada is not my first choice but I do need to get out of here. Can you send me some money? I will pay you back, I promise."

"Don't worry about that. I will send it to you in the morning. I can't wait to see you again, dear friend."

Chapter 13

Oh Canada

Adel arrives at the Vancouver International Airport in Canada. As he passes through customs, he sees Kamil waiting for him on the other side of the sliding doors. Adel didn't realize how happy he would be to see his friend again. When the glass doors slide open, he and Kamil run up and give each other a big hug. Kamil's hair is short and his face is clean shaven. He looks very well fed and most importantly he seems very happy.

They load his bags into Kamil's brown minivan. It is an older Toyota Sienna but in fairly good condition. Adel remembers the last time he had sat in his own shuttle van, the day the immigration officers grabbed him.

"Nice van, dude," Adel says as he gets into the passenger seat.

Kamil laughs. "Thanks. It actually belongs to my father-in-law. He has a Lexus and this van. He usually drives the Lexus and let's Ayca and me use this one." Kamil pulls out of the parking lot.

"That's right. How is married life?"

Kamil gives him a stiff smile. Ayca is a distant cousin who he had only known when he was a young boy. She had always been sweet to him as a child. She and her family immigrated to Canada when she was ten years old and he never saw her until his wedding day. He tells Adel how being married to Ayca was the best thing that happened to him. She feeds him well and takes good care of him. His father-in-law gave him a job at the family owned fast food restaurant in a busy mall in Vancouver so he is making a living. He studies English at the university during the day and works at the mall weeknights and on the weekends. Of course he has to say this. How could he tell Adel that he felt trapped and smothered by his annoying and anxious wife?

"That's great, brother. You deserve a good life and a good woman." Adel pats Kamil in the stomach. "You weren't kidding when you said she feeds you well." They both laugh.

Kamil drives Adel around Vancouver. "Hey, the skills you learned as a shuttle driver comes in handy. You are one of the best shuttle tour guides around…well except for me, of course," Adel says.

Kamil replies, "Well, I learned from the best."

As they drive through the city, Adel is astounded at the breathtaking scenery and most of all how clean the streets are. "You weren't kidding when you said Vancouver is beautiful. I have never seen such a green place before with so many beautiful trees and green grass everywhere. No wonder you love it here."

"YOU will love it here too, my brother," Kamil says. He was so happy to have his best friend staying with him again.

"We will soon see." Adel nods his head and smiles.

Kamil's wife's parents live in an older style six storey apartment building in the heart of South East Vancouver.

"This place is owned by my wife's parents. It's not that big but it is a home for us," he says as they ride up the elevator. The elevator creaks as it climbs up to the third floor. The smell reminds him of wet shoes.

When they enter the apartment, Adel is greeted with the smells of delicious food cooking on the stove. The living room is cozy with décor similar to his own home in Istanbul. He hears a familiar sound and turns to see the TV set which is playing his mother's favourite soap opera *Fatmagülün Suçu Ne (What is Fatmagul's Fault?)*.

"So you watch Turkish soap operas here in Canada?" Adel asks.

Kamil laughs. "You must have heard of satellite TV before. Come on now." Adel laughs too.

All of a sudden there is some chatter coming from the hallway and they are greeted by Kamil's wife, Ayca, a short plump dark haired woman dressed in a red long-sleeved sweater and a jean skirt that hangs just below her knees. Following behind her is Kamil's mother-in-law who, Adel notes, is an exact older version of Ayca.

A few minutes later, as if to make a grand entrance, Kamil's father-in-law enters the room. He eyes Adel suspiciously. His bushy grey uni-brow hangs over his eyes so Adel is unsure if he is frowning or if his eyebrow is in need of a good trim. Dressed in a brown button sweater and faded khaki pants and old leather slippers, it was clear how unimportant Adel's arrival was to him.

Ayca rushes over to Adel nearly toppling Kamil over the chair. "Welcome, Kamil has told us so much about you! How long will you be staying? Are you hungry? My mother and I cooked a big meal. Please, please come, come, sit." She pauses only to turn to Kamil—who is standing right behind her. At the top of her lungs she yells, "Kamil! Put Adel's bags behind the couch!"

Like a dutiful husband, Kamil politely smiles and picks up Adel's luggage and brings them behind the couch. Little does Adel know that this was where he was going to be sleeping.

Ayca bustles them inside.

Later at dinner, everyone is gathered at the dining table. Ayca and her mother have cooked a traditional meal and repeatedly remind Adel how lucky he is to be eating a home cooked meal. Adel is grateful to be welcomed to their table but he feels uncomfortable with Kamil's father-in-law's disapproving glare.

Kamil's wife is leading the conversation. "So you're not married yet? But why not? You are not getting any younger. You're so thin. You need a good woman to fatten your bones."

Kamil shakes his head. "Ayca, please stop. Adel has just arrived. You must not ask so many questions."

Adel smiles politely. He knows it is going to be a long night.

Kamil's father-in-law clears his throat. "Kamil says that you were in America before coming here to Canada. Why did you leave?"

Kamil looks over at Adel nervously. Adel smiles and pats him on the knee. "I missed Kamil too much."

Kamil's eyes widen but he turns to Ayca's father and tries to smile.

Ayca's father's face grows dark and he and his wife look at each other briefly. He shakes his head and continues. "We know your parents in Istanbul. They are very good people. We expect you to honour them even though you are here in Canada."

Adel replies quickly. "I always honour my parents."

Kamil leans over to his wife. "Ayca, why don't you go get the sweets that you made this morning?"

Ayca's face lightens up. "Oh, Ma helped too. A wife who cannot cook for her husband is not a good wife."

Adel smirks giving Kamil a look. Kamil smiles at his wife, elbowing Adel to behave. Ayca gets up and disappears into the kitchen to get the sweets.

Ayca's father leans forward and says to Adel, "You are a guest in my home but we expect you to help out around here. This is NOT a hotel!" He wags his finger at him.

Kamil and Adel look at each other. Before Adel can open his mouth to respond, Ayca returns with a big plate of baked goodies which she proudly places on the coffee table in front of them. Kamil offers a pastry first to Adel and then to his father-in-law who waves his hand impatiently to say no. Kamil takes a pastry for himself and he and Kamil take a big bite savouring the delicious flavor. They nod appreciatively at Ayca and her parents. Ayca's father rolls his eyes and sighs deeply.

Chapter 14

Not so easy

Adel finds it difficult to cope with life only after a few weeks at Kamil's home. The cramped size of the two bedroom apartment makes it difficult for him to find any privacy. The only moment he has for himself is when everyone goes to bed at night. That is the time when he pulls out the sofa bed in the living room and enjoys watching his favourite Turkish soap opera "Ezel". Even with the volume up, he can hear Ayca's father's snores from down the hall.

In the mornings, Kamil would get up early to attend his English classes at the university. Ayca's father leaves with him to open his restaurant. Adel has the day to go out and look for things to do or stay at the apartment with Kamil's wife and mother-in-law.

Since staying usually meant he had to hear Ayca's annoying yattering for the whole day, he usually made every effort to stay out of the apartment as much as he can. He tries exploring the city and uses the opportunity to find out what job opportunities are available for a man with his business skills.

Adel first tries the airport asking about how he can start his own shuttle van business. No one at the airport seems to know what he is talking about.

Adel finds the address of a local taxi cab company. Although he doesn't have an appointment, he shows up and looks for the owner in person rather than phoning the office. When he arrives, he speaks to the receptionist, an older woman probably in her sixties. He charms her to find out when the owner will be in the office. She explains that he will be back after lunch and that he is more than welcome to sit in the reception area until he arrives. Adel accepts the invitation and sits down waiting. One hour passes, then another. Finally it is almost four o'clock when a tall thin dark man comes through the door. The receptionist motions to Adel with her head that the man who just walked by was in fact the owner. Adel quickly jumps up and follows him out the door.

"Excuse me sir."

The owner stops and looks at Adel.

"I'm sorry to bother you but I was wondering if I could apply for a job as a taxi cab driver? I owned and operated my own shuttle van business in Los Angeles for the past year."

"Are you allowed to work in Canada?" the owner asks.

"Well, not exactly."

He points to a sample taxi cab license on the wall. He explains the paperwork and requirements for Adel to work as a cab driver. Adel shakes his head amazed at Canada's strict rules and regulations.

The owner is straightforward. He's been in the business long enough to know that it is difficult to get anywhere without the proper papers. There was no way in hell he was going to risk his business to help out some guy he didn't even know.

"Sorry, you need to have permanent residency status or a working visa. Then you need to get a Class 4 driver's license. Without these, there is nothing I can do for you."

Adel thanks him for his time and leaves.

On the weekend, Kamil sits at the dining table working on his homework assignments. Adel sits beside him looking through the newspaper. On the couch, Kamil's wife and his mother-in-law are preparing string beans in big baskets on their laps. Ayca's father sits beside them. Their eyes are glued to the Turkish soap opera on the TV set.

Adel leans forward to Kamil and says in a fake whisper, "What? Zenaib is secretly married to Milan, the servant's son?"

Ayca's face turns red. She snaps at Adel. "Shush, Adel! I'm trying to pay attention!" Ayca's mother turns and shushes them.

Ayca's father says angrily, "What is this? Can't you see that your mother is trying to watch her favourite soap opera?"

Ayca rolls her eyes and giggles. "You mean, you are trying to watch YOUR favourite soap opera dad."

Ayca's father raises his eyebrows and shakes his head. Adel and Kamil laugh to themselves.

Kamil lowers his voice. "Ayca and her parents are watching four Turkish soaps at the same time. I don't know why they watch them so religiously."

Adel smiles. "You know everyone back in Turkey is addicted to these soaps. Admit it, Kamil, you watch them too."

Kamil shakes his head feigning shock but then smiles. "How can I resist? People in love with people other than their husbands or wives? Gangsters working with the rich crooked politicians to steal from other rich crooked people. And the poor work for these people and live their lives through them. What's not to love watching this kind of drama?"

Adel nods his head in agreement. "I have to admit, I watch them too when your wife thinks I'm sitting in the living room reading my books. Just don't let her know!" They slap each other on the back and laugh. Kamil's father-in-law cries out asking Allah why his daughter's husband and his ungrateful friend will not let him enjoy a moment of peace in his own home.

* * *

Adel sits alone at the dining table looking through the newspaper at the classified advertisements. He finds an apartment for rent in the downtown area. He calls to find out how much it would cost for him to rent.

"Six hundred dollars a month for a bachelor suite?" Adel asks. He pauses, "Okay. Yes. Thank you." Adel crosses out another ad in the paper. The newspaper is covered with dark red lines from all the ads he has already crossed out.

The next day, Adel meets with an immigration lawyer. Adel is surprised. The lawyer looks like he just graduated from college. The advertisement in the newspaper says he gives thirty minutes free legal advice for those seeking to immigrate.

"Although it is possible to apply for permanent residency, you'll need to apply from Turkey. And it could take months or even years." He fidgets with his pen as he waits for Adel's response.

When he sees that Adel is not responding, he says, "There is also the Canadian Experience Class for people who have recent Canada work experience or have graduated and recently worked in Canada within two years of applying."

"And how much it costs for you to help me with the application?"Adel asks.

The lawyer replies, "Well our rates are two hundred dollars an hour, not including expenses and application fees."

Adel is shocked. "I should have known! Thank God, the first half hour is free! Two hundred dollars an hour? Your country won't let me work here so how do you expect me to pay you two hundred dollars an hour?" Adel gets up to leave.

The junior immigration lawyer softens his voice. "Sir, you can always fill out the application yourself. There are other resources out there such as immigration assistance services available for those who cannot afford to hire a lawyer. I'll have our secretary give you some leaflets with the information."

Adel realizes that he was only trying to be helpful. "Thank you. I appreciate that. I am sorry for ... for earlier."

The immigration lawyer nods his head. "I understand. This happens all the time."

Chapter 15

Questions that need answers

Kamil and Adel are walking through the streets of downtown Vancouver.

Adel is rambling. "You know if I could go back to LA, I'd get my money in Mirwan's apartment. I'd get my van..."

Kamil starts to say something which he soon regrets. "You might not need to go to LA."

Adel stops and turns to Kamil. He says, "What do you mean?"

Kamil clears his throat. "Well, I heard that he is here in BC. He's visiting his sister, my cousin, about five hours away. She just had a baby and their parents, brothers and sisters are all coming."

Adel says, "Is he staying at his sister's house?"

Kamil frowns. "Come on, Adel. I really shouldn't be telling you this. He is my cousin."

Adel scowls. "Your cousin backstabbed me. Am I not like your brother?"

Kamil says, "Yes, you are right. You are closer to me than my own brothers. And I have no respect for Mirwan. Never did. He was always hanging with the wrong crowd. But you know that Mirwan is still my cousin."

"Come on, man. You know I wouldn't do anything.... I just need to talk to him."

Kamil is silent.

Adel persists. "Please Kamil. I can't let this go until I talk to him."

Kamil finally nods his head. "Okay but I don't want anyone to know that I told you where he is. He is staying at his friend's place which is a few minutes from his sister's home."

Adel quickly adds, "I need you to come with me."

Kamil shakes his head. He couldn't believe Adel's nerve. "No. I won't do it. "

Adel becomes exasperated. "Come on, man…"

Kamil turns and walks ahead. "You can ask Mehmet from the restaurant to go with you."

The next day, after a long drive to Kelowna, Adel and Mehmet finally arrive in front of Mirwan's friend's house.

Adel turns to Mehmet. "Stay here. I won't be long." Mehmet nods his head. He was not one to argue too much. He admired Adel's confidence and stubbornness.

Adel looks at the address on the paper. He walks up to the house and rings the doorbell. Mirwan opens the door.

"Surprised to see me?" Adel's blood is boiling.

Mirwan tries to hide his nervousness. "What do you mean? I heard you were deported in LA."

Adel leans into his face. "And you had nothing to do with that?"

Mirwan shakes his head. "No, no… What do you mean?"

Adel grabs his shirt and pulls him towards him yelling in his face, "You traitor. Coward!" They struggle. "What happened to my van?!" Adel shakes Mirwan back and forth.

"Stop! I sold it! I didn't know if you were coming back. Stop!"

Adel shakes him harder. "Sold it? And my money… where is my money that was in your apartment?"

Mirwan feigns innocence. "What money? I don't know what you are talking about."

Adel points his finger in his face. "You ass…You knew about the money. You went through all my things. I knew it, you snake. Just answer me this… why? Why? Why did you do this to me? I was doing well with my business. I had plans. Why did you get me deported?"

Mirwan, the chicken that he really was, begins blubbering. "Because.. because I was jealous. It took me years to get to where I am. And you come here... with your smooth talk and white skin, blue eyes... If you were dark like me, you wouldn't have gotten to where you were... You were there because of me, you remember that, you son of a bitch."

Adel punches Mirwan in the jaw.

The front door opens and two men, possible friends of Mirwan's, come rushing in. They pull Adel off of Mirwan. They hold his arms back and Mirwan gets up from the ground and starts punching Adel in the gut. Adel struggles. Using all his energy, he head butts the man holding him and frees himself. He runs outside the door into the street.

One of the men pulls out a knife. "Get him!!"

Adel keeps running to the waiting car. Mehmet's eyes widen when he sees him.

Adel yells, "Let's go!" He jumps into the passenger side of the car. Mehmet sees the men running towards them. He changes the gear and presses the gas pedal to the ground. Wow, this was just like a scene from his favourite Turkish TV series. This may indeed be the most excitement he has had in his entire life. They speed down the street, leaving Mirwan and his two friends standing there swearing and shaking their fists at them.

"What was that all about?" Mehmet asks.

Adel, still shaky from the fights, says, "Never mind, just get us home... fast."

Hours later, Mehmet drops Adel off at Kamil's place. It is late at night and they are whispering so as not to wake Kamil's wife and parents. Kamil says, "What happened?" He sees the bruises on Adel's face.

"It was Mirwan."

Kamil is surprised. "Mirwan? You fought?"

"When I saw him," Adel says, "I just wanted to hurt him. Hurt him as much as he did to me."

Kamil shakes his head. "I can't believe Mirwan could put those bruises on you. You and I know what a coward he is."

Adel nods his head. "No, these aren't from Mirwan. They are from his friends."

Kamil's face grows dark. "You could have been killed. Those 'friends' of his are criminals."

"I know. I know... Thank God, I was able to escape."

Kamil still can't believe how stupid Adel was. "Now what?" he asks.

Adel pauses for a moment. "I wanted to get my money back from him."

"Why? For a couple hundred dollars?"

Adel shakes his head. "Not for a couple hundred... more like ten thousand dollars."

Kamil's eyes widen. Adel continues. "I worked hard for this money and there's no way I was going to leave it behind. I need it more than ever to start my life. Vancouver is so expensive to live here. There are no jobs for me. I can't use my degree to get a job because Canada does not recognize it."

Kamil pats him on the knee. "Okay, okay. I have another solution. Have you thought about my father-in-law's restaurant? I can get you a job there with me."

Adel shakes his head. "No, thanks. The last thing I want to do is work in that greasy hell hole." He folds his arms to stress his point.

Chapter 16

Greasy hell hole

The next morning, Adel is standing at the counter of Ayca's father's fast food restaurant in the food court of the mall. Covering his head is a hairnet and over his T-shirt and jeans is a white apron. If you could describe the look on his face, the word *miserable* would be an understatement. Robotically, he serves food to the never ending line up of customers. The restaurant is greasy and there is no room for him to move without bumping into Mehmet or Kamil. On top of the smell of burning oil, the escalating noise of people chattering in the mall is deafening.

Kamil's father-in-law is shaking his head and telling Adel loudly, "You are going too slow. Don't let me remind you that we have to meet the quota especially during the lunch period."

Adel nods his head and asks the next customer, "Yes, can I help you?"

The customer starts to order and then stops and changes his mind. Adel's patience is getting shorter and shorter.

"Sir, can you please tell me what you want to order?"

The man gives him a dirty look, "Hold your horses, buddy." He turns back to talk to his friends.

The line-up is getting longer and people are yelling, "Hey, hurry up! I gotta get back to work, dude!" A couple of women are yelling, "Yeah, what's going on? Let's go!"

Adel takes a deep breath. "Sir, please, if you are not ready, let me help the gentleman behind you."

The man behind the customer says, "Thanks!" and moves in front.

The man yells, "Hey!" He pushes the other man aside and yells at Adel. "Where's your manager?"

"What?"

The man says, "Can you understand English? I wanna talk to your manager!"

Adel tries to remain calm. "I understand English but I don't understand Pig-lish you big fat cow dung!"

The man raises his eye brows in shock. "What is a cow dung? Hey! You ASSHOLE!"

Adel sees red and jumps over the counter and shoves the man down. They start wrestling and rolling around. Customers are screaming and yelling. A huge commotion breaks out around them. Soon two security guards come running and pull each of them apart.

Kamil's father-in-law is running up to Adel. He yells. "How can you do this in my restaurant?" He pulls the sides of his hairs with his hands. "Enough! You are fired!"

Adel looks at him and rips off his hair net and apron. "No, you can't fire me because I QUIT!" Adel turns and walks angrily away.

Kamil runs after him. "Adel, please stop." He runs beside Adel.

Adel says angrily under his breath, "I am moving out of your apartment right now."

Kamil can't believe how awful this was turning out to be. "No, don't, Adel. You have no place to go."

Adel turns to him. "I can't live like this anymore. Thank you, I know you mean well but I have to move out."

"Where will you go?" Kamil asks.

Adel snaps. "I don't know yet but I'll be okay."

Kamil slows down and looks back at his very angry father-in-law. "I have to go back," he says.

Adel gives a sarcastic smile. "Yes, it's okay. Go back." What a coward. Adel disappears into the crowd.

Chapter 17

A king for a day

Adel packs his bags and moves out of Kamil's apartment. Luckily, Ayca and her mother were not home to give him the Spanish inquisition. He walks aimlessly down the street finally understanding that he has no place to stay. Adel walks by an expensive hotel. As he looks inside, he sees nicely dressed business men in suits and attractive ladies chatting with each other in the lobby. He pictures himself as one of them. Finally he decides that he was going in. He enters the hotel lobby and is greeted by a bell hop. The bell hop helps him with his bags. Adel smiles as he walks up to the check-in counter. He asks the pretty blonde hotel clerk for a room.

The hotel clerk does not raise her eyes. "We have a single room available."

Adel smiles at her. "How much?"

She continues typing on her keyboard. "Two hundred dollars a night."

Adel winces but looks around and sees how fancy the hotel is. "Yes. Good."

The hotel clerk looks up. Adel did not look like their hotel's typical clientele. "Will you be paying with Visa, Mastercard or Amex?"

Adel says proudly, "Cash. I have cash."

The hotel clerk nods her head slowly. "We also need a credit card to hold as a deposit."

Adel shakes his head. "I don't have credit card."

The clerk looks surprised. "I'm sorry, sir, but we do need a credit card."

Adel can't believe it. "I have cash. I pay for room now. Okay?" He slams his hand on the counter.

The clerk pauses and then walks away to talk to her supervisor.

The supervisor, a chic well-dressed man, comes up to the counter with a well-rehearsed smile. "Sir, we do need a credit card even if you are paying cash just as a protection in case there is any room damage or if you do not pay for the mini bar or services."

Adel pulls out his wallet and hands him ten one hundred dollar bills. "Is this enough for a deposit?"

The supervisor's eyebrows go up for a brief second. Then he puts on a cool smile. "Yes, sir. That is more than enough. We will keep this in our safe and return it to you when you check out." He turns to the clerk who is rolling her eyes and tapping her foot. "Please give this gentleman the deluxe suite." He smiles at Adel as the clerk gives him the keycard. "The bellhop will help you to your room." Adel enjoys the moment, nods and follows the bellhop to the elevators.

* * *

In his new luxurious suite, Adel takes photos with his cell phone so he can email them to his brothers back home. The room is large enough to fit his family and Kamil's family combined. He wanders around to inspect all the expensive furniture and paintings. After an hour of lounging around, he picks up his phone and tries to call Kamil's cell number. After a few rings, he reaches his voice mail message. Reluctantly, he calls Kamil's home.

Thankfully Kamil answers. "Where are you?" Kamil asks after recognizing his voice.

"At the Sheraton Plaza. I have a suite for a night. Come over."

Kamil had just come home from work. He was still wearing his hairnet and dirty work clothes. His father-in-law and his wife are seated on the opposite couch giving him the evil eye. He barks on the phone so as to impress his wife and father-in-law.

"What? That is very expensive I can imagine." His father-in-law nods his head in approval.

Adel replies, "It is just one night. I deserve one night to have a good night's sleep. Come over and we can act like tourists. Okay?"

Kamil turns away from his wife and father-in-law to hide his smile. It was just like old times. "Okay, yes we can be tourists for a day." He glances back and sees Ayca's sour face and her father's grim expression. "But you know my wife and her family are going to never forgive me."

"Hey, it will be worth it. At least you will have something to remember the next time your wife make you sleep on the sofa."

"Okay, sounds good." Kamil turns and smiles to himself. He almost forgot how much fun they used to have before he became a married man. He hangs up the phone.

"Why does Adel behave this way?!" Ayca cries out. Her father slams his newspaper on the table and asks the same question in a louder voice as if repeating it in a louder voice would make Kamil understand better.

"I'm worried too," Kamil says. "I will call his parents for help."

Ayca and her father shake their heads in disgust.

An hour later, Adel and Kamil are driving around the city just like the first days when they arrived in Hollywood.

Kamil asks, "What are you going to do now?"

Adel shakes his head. "Honestly, I do not know. I think that my dream of opportunity was only just a dream."

Kamil realizes it is a good time to ask Adel. "Why don't you do something different?"

Adel frowns. "Like what?"

Kamil smiles broadly. "Take English lessons with me at the university."

Adel rolls his eyes. "And what is that going to do for me?"

Kamil wasn't going to let his pessimism stop him. "Give yourself a change. The university is beautiful. There is different kind of people there. People who have dreams like you. Young people with life."

Adel nods slowly. He half laughs. "Is my English so bad, Kamil?"

Kamil says, "No, of course not. But you can do better. And of course writing in English. That is our weakness."

Adel can see that Kamil was dead serious about this. And hey, what did he have to lose? "Okay, you convinced me, brother. Tomorrow, I go to register. How much is classes?"

Kamil says, "Well, my full time program costs forty-two hundred dollars for a 12 week program."

Adel didn't believe Kamil could ever have that kind of money.

"How did you pay for this?"

Kamil smiles sheepishly. "I borrowed the money from my father-in-law."

Adel laughs. "Hmmm. You really got your nuts in his vice." They laugh together, knowing that this was the truth.

Later that night, the two friends hang out at the hotel's dance club. Many young women are making their moves on Adel and Kamil. While Kamil tries to politely keep his distance, Adel is flirting with all of them, drunk with happiness—and a dozen bottles of beer which he had been guzzling down all evening.

One cute brunette pulls him onto the dance floor. Her friend grabs Kamil's arm and soon the four of them are dancing together.

"Where are you from?" the brunette asks Adel.

Adel laughs. "I'm from Russia."

The woman grinds up closer to him. "Ahh, I knew that was a Russian accent."

Kamil is also dancing but he keeps shaking his head when the brunette comes too close to Adel. Soon the girl and Adel start to kiss. This gives the brunette's friend the courage to try to kiss Kamil. He turns his face away from her. He turns towards Adel who is in a lip-lock with his dance partner. He pulls the kissing couple apart.

"Let's go, Adel," Kamil says.

Adel laughs. "Come on... I'm having so much fun."

Kamil says firmly while pulling Adel's arm, "That's enough fun for tonight. Let's go."

Adel makes a face but half realizes that he is not feeling well. He lets Kamil pull him away from the woman.

"Hey! Where you going?" she cries out.

"Call me!" Adel says half drunk and he motions with his hand to call him.

The brunette says, "But you didn't leave me your—"

The men are too far to hear the rest. Finally outside on the street, Adel starts singing at the top of his lungs. Kamil shakes his head and decides it is time to call it a night.

Chapter 18

Facing reality

In the hotel room, Adel and Kamil are eating pistachio nuts and smoking a water pipe.

"That was the most fun I had since... well since we first arrived in LA," Adel says.

Kamil nods. "Yes, this was fun." They both are mellowing down now. "What time is it?" Kamil asks.

Adel shrugs. "I don't know and don't care."

Kamil checks the TV. "Oh no, it's three a.m. My wife is going to kill me."

Adel says, "Just call her and tell her you are with me. Stay over tonight. There are two huge beds here."

Kamil looks reluctant but then says, "Well, I'm the man of the family. She better accept that." He picks up the phone.

Adel half listens to his pathetic friend who first starts out apologetic to his wife but then ends up in an angry defensive tone. He hangs up. He says, "Well, if she thinks she can tell me who my friends are, she has her head screwed on wrong."

Adel laughs. "See, my friend, this is why I did not want to have an arranged marriage."

Kamil pauses, and then says, "Adel, I don't know how to tell you this."

Adel senses impending bad news. "Tell me what?"

"Your father called me looking for you today," Kamil says, "so I told him that you had moved out. When I couldn't tell him how to contact you, he said to tell you this. Your mother is very worried about you. You had not called them since you came to Canada."

Adel sighs. "Yes, I know. But what to tell them? That I'm miserable? That I can't get myself even a job?"

Kamil continues. "Well, your father said that he had spoken to your Grand Uncle."

Adel frowns.

"He asked your Grand Uncle to help you. Grand Uncle thought about it and has made a decision. He has arranged for you to marry his granddaughter. She's here in Vancouver for three years now."

Adel's eyes widen in shock. "What?! He can't do that!"

Kamil pauses. "Well, according to your father, your Grand Uncle is flying here with your cousins this weekend. They want my wife to arrange to have his granddaughter meet with you on Monday. By next Sunday, you will be married."

Adel jumps up completely furious. "I refuse! Grand Uncle cannot do this to me!"

Kamil says calmly, "I do not know if you have a choice. Your parents have already agreed to this and they have already spoken to your cousin's parents. They have already paid the dowry."

Adel looks more surprised. "With what? They don't have any money."

Kamil pauses again. "Your father gave a piece of his land over to your Grand Uncle. In return, your Grand Uncle has released half of your father's properties to him so that he can split these with you and your brothers. He has also given your father some of the money that is owed to him from the inheritance. Your father is going to send this to you so that you can use it to buy a home. But I don't think it is enough to buy a home here. You could use it to take English courses. That would really help you out."

Adel is beginning to understand now that the arrangement of his marriage is only the tip of the iceberg.

"So that means if I do not go ahead with this, then my family will pay the price for it?"

Kamil sighs and nods his head. "Come on, man. Maybe this is a good thing. A good woman might be what you need to change your life around."

Adel nods slowly. "Yes, maybe you are right…"

Kamil laughs. "I'm going to sleep now. I usually am in bed by 11 o'clock."

Adel agrees. "Okay." They climb into their beds and shut the lights.

"Kamil," Adel says after a few minutes.

Kamil mumbles, "Hmm?"

"Do you remember that woman I told you about...the one in LA?"

Kamil turns over. "Nooo...I'm tired. Sleepy..."

Adel half talks to himself, "I thought about her a lot when I was in the detention. I was supposed to see her before she left LA. I never had a chance to say good-bye." Kamil mumbles not hearing Adel's rambling. "I wanted to find her but I don't know if she would even remember me. Just a shuttle van driver... But it was such a nice kiss..." He drifts off to sleep.

PART TWO

An Arrangement

Chapter 19

Grand Uncle

Adel's Grand Uncle sits awkwardly in Kamil's living room on a chair which is much too small for him. His stocky build along with his obesity makes him the size of two huge men or a baby elephant as Adel always says to Kamil. Beside him stands his bodyguard overlooking the sheikh, a shy small man who seemed to shrink into his suit—a suit perhaps borrowed from a close relative. Adel and his father sit on the love seat across from them. If they could sit any closer, they'd be Siamese twins, Adel thinks to himself.

Grand Uncle clears his throat, a sign that the formalities were commencing. "I have the immigration lawyer papers for Yonka's petition to apply for your status in Canada. After you two are married, the paperwork will be submitted. We are doing this as requested by your father. However, I expect you to honour your wife Yonka, my granddaughter. If there is any reason for me to doubt this, we will stop the application."

Adel replies, "I will honour my father's request. But just to let you know that I have no desire to have my status in Canada be the result of this marriage. I will try to be a good husband."

Grand Uncle continues. "After the wedding, you will move into Yonka's apartment which I bought for her years ago. The paper is in her name. She has been paying the mortgage but now you will also contribute to the mortgage."

Adel looks at Kamil with a frown and turns to his Grand Uncle. "If I am going to pay the mortgage, should not the paper of the house also be in my name?"

The Grand Uncle bursts into laughter. "Consider it rent. If you want to have your name on the paper, pay me the one hundred thousand dollar deposit and the money Yonka has already paid the bank. And on top of that, we will get a real estate agent to estimate the property and you can ask the bank for mortgage for that amount."

Adel turns red. "I see. Please retract my earlier request."

Grand Uncle says, "Enough talk. Let's proceed with signing."

The sheikh hands a gold pen to the Grand Uncle and the body guard turns the papers towards him. The Grand Uncle scribbles his signature on the document and then shoves the papers towards Adel. The sheikh hands Adel the pen and gives him a nod, a signal for him to sign the papers.

Adel takes the pen, hesitates for a moment and glances over at his father. His father nods his head as well, silently telling him to hurry up.

Adel takes a deep breath and signs his name on the paper, sealing the deal—the arrangement made between his father and his Grand Uncle is now complete.

* * *

Kamil motions to his wife. She nods and leaves the room. After a few minutes, she brings in a tall full figured young woman dressed in a royal blue shiny gown with long sleeves and pearl buttons on her neck. Her hair is covered in a darker blue chiffon scarf. Pale peach gloss adds a shine to her lips and her hazel eyes have only a touch of brown eye shadow to accent them. Adel's Grand Uncle nods approvingly and he motions for her to sit. A large chair had been prepared for her, covered in white silk cloth and pillows. It was Ayca's way of trying to make the event more regal.

Grand Uncle clears his throat again. "Yonka, you remember your cousin Adel." She looks into her lap and nods.

* * *

Years ago when Adel and Kamil were young boys, Yonka used to stand and watch them play. She was a tall thin, awkward-looking girl. One day, Adel and Kamil were playing cards in the yard which was shared with his Grand Uncle and his family.

She walks up to them with her nose in the air, her hands on her hips. "You know you aren't permitted to play cards. It's forbidden! I'm going to tell my grandfather."

Adel ignores her. "Come on, Kamil, show me your hand."

Kamil laughs and puts down his cards.

Yonka softens her voice. "Let me play."

Kamil looks up at her. "I thought you said that it's forbidden to play cards."

Adel smirks while Yonka makes a face. Then she gives a sly smile. "Well, if you let me play, I won't tell Grandfather."

Adel gives Kamil a "No way, you're not going to fall for that again" look.

Kamil says, "Well, this game is not for girls."

Yonka stomps her foot. "Let me play or else!" Adel stands up and looks her in the eye (she is slightly taller so he has to look up).

"Or else what?" he asks.

"I don't think you'd like to know..." Yonka chuckles to herself.

Adel turns around. "Hmph... What a donkey. Kamil, let's find another place to play." Kamil shrugs and starts picking up the cards.

Suddenly, Yonka whirls around and runs to the garden digging her hands in the soil and smashing the dirt into her face and dress. She howls and cries in a loud voice, "Grandfather!!! Mother!!!"

Adel and Kamil, stunned by her actions, stand frozen watching her. Suddenly the women servants and Adel's Grand Uncle come running out to see what is happening. Grand Uncle cries out, "What on earth is all this noise? What happened to you, granddaughter?"

Yonka, now slumped on the ground, starts weeping and pointing her finger at Adel. Adel and Kamil frown and look at each other.

Yonka's mother comes running to her. "What happened, Yonka? Who did this to you?"

Yonka looks up with tears flowing from her eyes. She whimpers, "Adel and Kamil beat me up and pushed me into the dirt when I told them that it is forbidden to play cards."

Grand Uncle turns around, his eyeballs bulging from the sockets. He cries out, "How dare you beat on a girl and your cousin? And gambling in my house?!" He walks over to Adel, picks up his slipper and proceeds to give him a good smacking.

"Stop! Grand Uncle! Stop! I had nothing to do with this!" Adel cries out.

Grand Uncle, his face purple with anger cries out, "Liar! Liar! Get your good for nothing selves out of here. You are going to be cleaning the chicken coop and mopping all the floors for a month!"

He whirls around and points at Kamil yelling, "And you Kamil, don't come by this house until your father comes to apologize personally for this. Have you no shame?"

In all the commotion, Yonka smiles secretly to herself as her mother walks her back into the house.

* * *

The wedding ceremony finally begins. It is a grand affair considering the fact that there are only forty-five guests. Most of the guests are the staff who work at

Kamil's father-in-law's fast food restaurant and the
rest are a few family members from Adel and Kamil's
family. Adel and Yonka are sitting awkwardly by
themselves at the head table. Yonka is dressed in a
lavish red wedding gown with gold trim. On her head is
an opulent head dress that looks more like a crown
laden with large colourful jewels. Modern Turkish
weddings usually have the bride dressed in a Western
style white wedding gown so Adel was a bit surprised
to see his bride dressed in red. In the 1800s, it was
traditional for a Turkish bride to wear red and
sometimes the colour is used as a fashion statement,
but seeing Yonka in red on their wedding day made
him think her intent was far from being traditional. At
the bride's family's table, Grand Uncle is gulping down
his wine like it was water. With the alcohol in his
system, he feels like the ladies' man he imagines himself
to be. He makes sure every woman at his table saves a
dance for him. The guests, awed by the extravagance,
drink in every minute of this one of a kind celebration.
And why not? Who would say no to free food, drink
and entertainment—Turkish style?

A sexy belly dancer weaves her way into the crowd while the band plays a festive Turkish wedding song. Kamil anxiously looks over at Adel who is making attempts at idle conversation with his new bride. He gives him a nod of encouragement when he catches his eye. Adel nods back in return. He raises his glass to Yonka who smiles shyly back at him.

Chapter 20

Honeymoon is over

At a few minutes past midnight, the wedding party comes to an end, and the guests watch as the newlyweds are escorted outside to a black limousine. Yonka and Adel wave to everyone and soon are whisked away into the night. Where will they be going for their honeymoon, some ask each other. Hawaii? Las Vegas? Paris or Rome? Little do they know that the limousine's destination is only a few minutes away to a posh high rise apartment in the West End—Yonka's condominium and Adel's new home.

When they arrive, Yonka tells the driver to park in the driveway in front of the building. He does as he is told. Once parked, he rushes out and helps Yonka out of the car.

Adel soon realizes that the honeymoon is over before it had even begun. He climbs out of the car, unsure of what to do next. The driver hands him his suitcase. He recalls how once not long ago, he himself was a driver, dropping his clients off hoping to receive a good tip for his hard work. He reaches for his wallet and hands the driver fifty dollars and tells him to keep the change. The driver thanks him profusely and offers to carry his suitcase into the building. Yonka was not going to let him do that.

"You may go now," Yonka orders the driver. He gives Adel a weak smile and returns back to the car.

Adel shakes his head as he follows Yonka into the building. The lobby of the building is impressive with twenty foot ceilings and marble floors. Nothing surprising since her grandfather was a man who loved to show off his wealth. They ride in the elevator silently up to the third floor. Adel wonders why his Grand Uncle didn't have his precious granddaughter living in the penthouse suite. Little did he know that Yonka was afraid of heights. She had a recurring nightmare of falling down from a high place. She always woke up in a cold sweat, wondering if this was a premonition.

Yonka quickly steps out of the elevator. She hurries down the hallway and turns around the corner. Still pulling his suitcase out of the elevator, he can hear her fumbling with her keys. By the time he reaches the door, she has already entered the apartment. He follows her inside.

He looks around but his new bride is not in sight. He notes that the suite is just as impressive as the lobby entrance with high ceilings, large living area and modern stylish furniture. He notices the coffee table is littered with nail polish bottles, paperback books, and dirty plates. On the sofa, a pink sweater is draped on the arm rest. On the dining table, there are half eaten pastries on plates and a half drunken glass of wine.

"Well, that was interesting," Yonka says. Adel is startled and almost trips over his suitcase.

Yonka removes her head dress and her high heel shoes and tosses them on the floor. He watches her walk down to the hallway with a confident sway as she enters a room at the end. Will he and his new bride be having their honeymoon in there? Adel stands alone awkwardly in the living room with his suitcase beside him—waiting. A few minutes pass when finally the bedroom door swings open. Yonka comes out dressed in black leggings and a tight tank top, the top of her bust spilling out of the neckline. In her arms she is carrying blankets and a pillow. She walks past him as she drops the bundle of bedding on the couch. Adel shakes his head in disbelief.

"What is this?" he asks.

"Let's just get this straight out on the table. I'm not that little kid you used to tease and call donkey back in grade school. And I'm definitely not the girl my grandfather wants me to be." She glares at him.

"So you don't want this arranged marriage?" he asks.

"Not any more than you do."

Adel pauses. "So…"

"So, you stay out of my way and I'll stay out of yours. Oh and at the first of the month, you have to give me your share of the bills. You *should* be paying for all of it since you are technically my husband. But whatever." She turns around and picks up her purse from the couch. She rummages inside.

Adel nods. "I guess you are not a traditional wife who stays at home and let the husband make the rules."

Yonka laughs. "Isn't that the truth?" Her hand still in her purse finally pulls out a cigarette and a lighter. She turns towards him and lights up her cigarette. Adel makes a face. With a smirk on her lips, she comes up close to him and blows smoke towards him. He turns and coughs.

She looks him up and down, inspecting his features like he was a prize cow. Finally she says, "You did grow up to be somewhat nice looking."

He frowns.

She continues. "But I bet you're still the boring Mr. Know-It-All I remember when we were children."

He says, "I do not remember you well."

She reaches over and caresses his face. She nuzzles her face on his shoulder and places hot kisses on his neck. He stiffens and turns away. This doesn't stop her. In a husky whisper she says, "This is our wedding night, my sweet Turkish husband." She pushes him down on the couch and climbs on top of him, sitting provocatively on his lap.

Who does she think she is? He stands up suddenly causing Yonka to lose her balance and fall to the ground.

"Hey! Is this how you treat your bride?" She tries to pick herself up from the floor.

He looks down at her in disgust. "Act like a respectable woman. Have you no shame?" He picks up his suitcase and walks down the hallway.

"Where do you think you're going?" Yonka asks. She follows after him. There are two doors on each side of the hall. He flings open the first one only to see that it is a laundry room. He opens the second door which leads him into a small bedroom with a twin size bed. The room is cluttered with boxes, shopping bags and clothes. Shaking his head, he drops his suitcase on the floor. He gathers all the items on the bed and carries them into the room Yonka had entered earlier. On the wall above a king size bed, he sees a large portrait of Yonka on the wall confirming that this indeed was her bedroom. He walks across the room to double glass doors opening into an enormous walk-in closet. The closet is bigger than the cell he had at the detention centre. Still carrying Yonka's things, he walks inside looking for a place to dump them. He trips over one of many pairs of shoes strewn on the floor. The boxes slip from his hand and land into piles of clothes and handbags in the corner. He is amazed beyond belief. How many shoes or purses can one woman own?

Behind him Yonka yells, "Do not touch my stuff! What do you think you are doing?"

Adel turns around angrily and looks her in the eye. "The other room is mine. Your stuff stays in your room. You stay out of MY way and I'll stay out of yours. You get in my face and see how miserable I can make your life!"

Yonka steps back in shock. She pauses for a bit. Then she makes a face and snarls, "Well that's a real nice way to start our honeymoon, husband of mine."

Before Adel can say another word, the phone rings and Yonka turns around and walks back to the living room.

* * *

Later, in his new room, Adel tosses and turns, trying to fall asleep. Yonka's loud laughter and chatter from her room makes all his efforts pointless. Grey wafts of cigarette smoke creep under his door and fill the room. Adel checks his cell phone. It is two a.m. in the morning. He sighs heavily, shakes his head, turns over and puts the pillow over his head. Maybe if he pushed it hard enough, he could smother himself to sleep.

Chapter 21

Online venture

One afternoon a few weeks after the wedding, Adel comes home with Kamil carrying a big "Best Buy" shopping bag. Adel is like a boy ready to open up his presents on his birthday. Yonka comes out of the kitchen and looks curiously at them.

"What's in the bag?"

Adel gives her a cool smile. "Wouldn't you like to know?" She scowls but doesn't leave. She watches intently as Adel and Kamil empty the bag on the coffee table.

"Come on, open it," Kamil says. Adel opens a box and brings out a bright shiny new fifteen inch laptop. Adel carefully takes out all the items from the box. Yonka reaches over to touch the laptop. Adel pulls it away from her reach.

"You don't want to show me your new toy?" she asks.

Kamil chuckles. "Ask nicely and maybe he will let you play with it."

Adel rolls his eyes. "Whatever. Come on, Kamil, let's go to my room." Kamil picks up the shopping bag and follows Adel who has his laptop under his arm. Yonka crosses her arms on her chest and pouts.

* * *

Inside Adel's bedroom, Adel shows Kamil how to surf the internet, clicking and typing excitedly. Kamil looks over his shoulder amazed at what he sees on the screen.

Kamil says, "So you think you can make money doing this?"

Adel turns to him. "Of course. Isn't this fantastic? I can run my own business right here from my room."

Kamil says, "But where will you store the items you want to sell?"

Adel smiles. "I won't have to store anything. This is the beauty of it. It's called drop-shipping."

Kamil says, "Ok. It is all new to me. I can't wrap my head that you can sell something without even seeing it."

Adel says, "It is the age we live in, my brother. We have to... hmmm... how do Canadians say... *Go with the flow?*"

Chapter 22

Fate would have it

Adel and Kamil walk around the university campus. They are enjoying school life together just as they did when they were in high school. On this day, Adel and Kamil are sitting on a bench outside their school building. They are busy chatting with each other about Adel's business and the surprising amount of money he has generated.

After a while, Kamil says, "So forget about the business for now...how is married life? It seems that you and Yonka are getting along better."

Adel shakes his head. "It was a mistake."

Kamil is surprised. "It has only been one month. You have to give it a chance."

Adel frowns. "You don't understand. Yonka is not what you think she is. She's not like your wife. She was only pretending in front of Grand Uncle. Living at her place is worse than the detention."

Kamil nods his head slowly and then says softly, "So the gossip is true."

Adel stops and looks at Kamil. "You knew? And you convinced me to do this?"

Kamil shakes his head. "I didn't know anything. My wife did mention that when your Grand Uncle sent her here three years ago, it was to avoid having a scandal exposed. Her parents came to your Grand Uncle to send her away to the West to stay with her aunt."

Adel glowers at Kamil.

"I thought it was just pure gossip," Kamil says. "Women in the Turkish community gossip with each other all the time. I didn't take it too seriously."

Adel can't believe his ears. "She is driving me crazy. She smokes in the house. She drinks. She is messy, loud and arrogant," he says. "When she was a kid, I couldn't stand her then. But then her parents moved to Ankara and I never saw her again until now."

Kamil sighs. "Sorry, brother. What is going to become of this?"

Adel says, "I don't know. Really I don't know."

* * *

They walk into their class and nod hello to their classmates as the class starts. The students look at the front and whisper to each other. Adel and Kamil stop chatting and look up. Adel's eyes widen in disbelief. Standing at the front of the class is Nora, dressed in a stylish dress suit.

"Good morning, class. I will be your teacher for the rest of the term. My name is Nora Lee Morgan. I am back from sabbatical leave. Some of you I've already had the privilege of having in my class before.

As Nora continues speaking to the class, Kamil elbows Adel and whispers, "She's hot."

Adel is stunned.

Nora says to the class, "Let's spend a few minutes introducing yourselves to me."

The students begin to say their names and Kamil says to Adel, "Hey, what's the matter with you?"

Adel leans towards Kamil. "That's the girl…"

"What girl?" Kamil asks.

Adel whispers loudly, "The girl from LA."

Kamil nods slowly understanding now. "You mean you kissed her?"

"Excuse me, gentlemen," Nora says to them.

Adel and Kamil face the front like two children caught exchanging quiz answers in class. Nora smiles at both of them ready to say a few words when her smile leaves her face.

"Sorry, Ma'am. My name is Kamil. It is nice to meet you," Kamil says.

Adel clears his throat. "My name is Adel Emre. I am very happy to meet you…"

After a brief moment, Nora smiles hesitantly. "Thank you. It is a pleasure to meet both of you." She continues talking to the rest of the students.

* * *

When the class ends, Adel says to Kamil, "Go ahead. I'll meet you later."

Kamil nods, grabs his books and leaves.

Adel turns to Nora when the classroom is empty.

Nora puts her papers into her briefcase. Not meeting Adel's eyes, she says, "Funny, I thought I'd never see you again."

"I was hoping the opposite," Adel says quietly.

Nora shakes her head and walks to her desk. "What do you mean? I gave you my phone number and waited for you to call. But you never did. So I figured, oh well… it was a nice memory but nothing more."

Adel comes up behind her and holds her elbow. She looks down at his hand and then he brings her face into his hands. He looks deep into her eyes.

"I was wondering if the feelings I had the last time I saw you were just my imagination."

She takes a breath.

He continues. "But now that you are here, the feelings are here and even stronger."

She pulls away and turns around. "Well, maybe it's too late for this now. Opportunities come and go."

Adel pulls her back to him. "Please let me explain."

She shakes her head. "There is no need for explanations."

Adel interrupts. "Yes, there is and I want to give you one. A few days after I met you, I was arrested and placed in an immigration detention centre for thirty days and then later deported back to Istanbul."

Nora's mouth opens.

He continues. "I thought about you every day I was in the detention. I wanted to call you but your number was not with me."

Nora nods slowly. "So that's the reason…hmm… I really just thought it was nothing to you… I mean the moment we had."

Adel shakes his head. "It was everything to me," he says. "Nora… It *is* everything to me."

Nora shakes her head and pulls away again. "I think we have to stop this."

"Why?"

She pauses. "I'm engaged to be married."

Adel repeats slowly, "Married…"

She continues. "My ex-boyfriend and I got back together a few months ago."

Adel looks down and hides his hand into his pocket remembering his ring. "I see," Adel says, "do you love him?"

Nora is surprised with the bluntness of his question. "Of course I do. What kind of a question is that?"

Adel sighs. "I have something to tell you too." At that moment, students begin to enter the room for the next class.

"I will talk to you later. Okay?"

Nora nods. "Yes. We can talk. We can still be friends."

Adel says sarcastically, "Yes... friends."

He turns and walks out of the room. Nora watches him leave as the students for her next class enter the room.

Chapter 23

Yonka

Yonka works at the Hyatt Regency Hotel as a catering and events manager. Her colleagues in the Events department are her closest friends. Susan, the events coordinator, is an Irish Canadian in her mid-thirties. Jenny, the marketing manager, is a twenty-five year old Chinese Canadian. Finally her closest friend, Guy, the catering manager, is a colourful Austrian in his mid-fifties. Fridays are saved for their weekly get-together of drinking vodka and smoking "medicinal" weed. Guy has acute rheumatoid arthritis and his hippie doctor friend prescribed him medicinal marijuana to help ease his pain. Call it sharing some natural medicine with your friends, Guy always says.

Susan turns to Yonka. "So does Mario know that you're married now?" She passes the joint to Yonka.

"Well, no....How can I tell him that?" Yonka giggles. She passes the joint to Jenny. No one notices that she is not smoking with them.

Jenny says, "So he still thinks you and him are going out?" She takes a few quick puffs and hands the joint to Susan.

Yonka rolls her eyes. "It's a little more complicated than that."

"How complicated is it to say, 'I am married?'" Susan asks. She puffs the joint several times until Guy glares at her. She sheepishly hands the joint back to him.

Guy says, "Don't you think he deserves to know?"

Yonka turns red. "When he moved out of here three months ago to work in Dubai, I thought it was over."

"And so he called you to say that he missed you and can't live without your bullcrap? Heard it all before, honey." He gives the joint the last few puffs and puts the butt into the ashtray.

Yonka smiles bitterly. "Then I find out a week after he left that I'm pregnant." She reaches down to touch her belly.

Susan laughs. "And so is that why you agreed to the arranged marriage thing?"

Yonka nods. "Yeah, crazy huh? But a part of me thought that Mario would come back if I told him."

"And so you told him?" Jenny asks.

"When he contacted me, ironically it was the day of the wedding. I couldn't believe he wanted to get back together."

Guy interrupts. "So did you tell him?"

Yonka shakes her head. "I tried to... but then...It is too complicated. I don't know."

"What about your 'husband'?" Jenny asks. "Does he know?"

Yonka laughs. "No. I want to wait until I get things figured out."

Susan shakes her head. "So you're going to make him think that he's the baby's daddy?"

"Well it's kind of difficult," Yonka says, "since we haven't even consummated the marriage." All three friends laugh out loud.

"What?" Guy chirps. "And how in the world do you expect hubby to believe he's the daddy?"

Yonka says, "Hey, it's not like I didn't try. I've tried to seduce him. But he gets so traditional on me and keeps saying, *'Become a respectable woman before you come near me again, woman.'*"

"Whoa... a guy who says no to free sex and from his legitimate wife?" Susan laughs.

"Are you sure he's not gay?" Guy adds in a matter-of-fact tone. The women break out into uncontrollable giggles.

The front door opens and Adel and Kamil enter the smoke-filled apartment. Adel sees Yonka sitting on the far chair dressed in a tight black mini dress with a wine glass in her hand. Her friends are facing her, unaware of his or Kamil's presence. Kamil looks over at Yonka and waves. He has met Yonka's friends a few times before at other functions and get-togethers.

Kamil says, "Hello Yonka." Her friends all turn to look.

Guy whispers to the women, "Wow, Yonka, you didn't mention that your husband was such a hottie. Hey, I'd do him!"

Susan laughs. "After me, baby."

Jenny chimes in. "Maybe he'd like a foursome."

Yonka glares at them. "Hey, that's my husband you're talking about here."

Guy laughs. "Whatever, Yonka...whatever."

Adel can't believe that Yonka would disrespect him in front of her friends. He points his finger at Yonka. "If you want to smoke that stuff, do it somewhere else."

Yonka raises her eyebrows and stands up. "Oh yeah? And what???"

Adel opens his mouth and then says under his breath, "Don't test me, Yonka. Like I said before, stay out of my way and I'll stay out of yours. Cross me and you'll regret it."

Yonka makes a face and then turns to her friends. "Come on, let's go. Reservations were for seven p.m."

Guy and Jenny get up from the couch.

Jenny slithers up close to Adel. "Yonka, where's your manners? Aren't you going to introduce us?"

Yonka says, "Oh sure... This is Susan, Jenny, Guy... We work together at the hotel. This is Adel, my husband. Come on, guys, let's go."

Guy comes up to Adel to shake his hand. "Very nice to meet you."

Adel shakes his hand reluctantly. "Nice to meet you..."

Yonka says again, "Okay guys, let's go."

"What's the rush?" Susan says. "Why don't we order in and you know hang out here? It would be nice to get to know Adel a little bit more."

Adel coughs into his hand. "Actually, I'm having dinner at Kamil's. Thank you for the invitation. Come on, Kamil, let's go."

Kamil looks at Adel with surprise and then regains his composure. "Yes, you know the wife gets really upset if we are late for one of her delicious home cooked meals." He winks at Yonka. They turn and leave.

"Wow, that was the fastest exit ever." Guy chuckles to himself.

Susan elbows her. "You know, Yonka, if I were you, I'd forget about Mario and concentrate on your husband."

Jenny giggles. "Is he really your cousin?"

"Yes he is."

"I can't see the resemblance," Jenny says. The newlyweds were like night and day. They seemed to have nothing in common with each other.

Susan and Guy laugh along with Jenny. Yonka doesn't understand the inside joke and looks confused.

She finally says, "Mario wants me to go to Dubai."

"No way!" Jenny shakes her head.

Susan nods slowly. "Now I know why you say that this is complicated."

Guy looks at the door. "Honey, you've got the big catch right here and you're just too blind to see it."

Chapter 24

A different perspective

After the swift departure from Yonka's pot party, Kamil drives Adel to his apartment.

"I can't believe this woman," Adel says. "She is smoking weed in the house and drinking alcohol with her friends."

Kamil nods his head. "She is definitely not the traditional woman she appeared to be at the wedding."

"That's it. I can't take this crap anymore. I'm going to annul the marriage."

"What?" What is Adel talking about?

"What do you mean 'what'?" Adel snaps.

Kamil says, "But you remember that your Grand Uncle and your father made an agreement with each other. Why would you ruin everything for your family?"

Adel shakes his head, "I can't believe you are saying this. I can't live like this. I want to have my own life."

Kamil frowns. "You know, Adel, you never change."

Adel is surprised that Kamil is not taking his side on this. "What? What are you trying to say?"

"You always think about yourself," Kamil says. "Your life, your dreams, your goals. You don't think of your family or your friends."

Adel is stunned. "I really don't understand why you are saying this," he says. "Of course I care about my family. I send them money. I did this arranged marriage thing because of them."

Kamil half laughs. "Oh come on, Adel. You did this arranged marriage thing only because it was convenient. You needed a way to stay in Canada and this is the ticket. Your father knew this and that's why he arranged for this."

Adel scowls. "Oh that is *so* wrong. I don't care if they deport me tomorrow. I want to get out of this circus of a marriage."

Kamil wasn't going to let Adel have the last word. "You know, if you went into the marriage with the right intentions, maybe you could get Yonka to come around. She's being influenced by foreigners and she needs someone like you to set her straight. She IS your cousin after all."

"I don't *care* if she is my cousin. What did Grand Uncle ever do for my family?" Adel clenches his fists. "I hate my cousins. They are all selfish, ungrateful cockroaches. They are always getting things without even having to work for it."

Kamil smirks. "Yeah, I heard it all before, Adel. Your horrible Grand Uncle and your weak father. Didn't it ever occur to you that your father isn't weak?" Kamil asks. "That maybe what you see is weak is really that he is a very fair and kind man who is not greedy like your uncles and aunts. If your dad was just like them fighting for land and money from your grandfather's inheritance, maybe you and your brothers and sisters might end up just like your horrible cousins."

Adel's jaw opens to say something and then he stops.

Kamil continues. "And your Grand Uncle was like a secondary father to your father when your grandfather died. He had to run the family business and take care of his family and your father like he was his own son."

Adel scowls. "Oh sure... my Grand Uncle took the opportunity to take the money from my grandfather's business and save it all for himself and his own children," he says. "He took care of my father? He treated him like he was an orphan servant. My father always got the scraps. And my father never said anything."

"Yes but your father was only a very young boy when your grandfather died," Kamil says. "How do you expect him to say anything to his uncle who was a grown man with his own family?"

Adel shakes his head. "Yeah, and my Grand Uncle took advantage of the fact that my father was a young boy and never let him think for himself."

"Yes, but like I said, what you see as your father's weakness is actually his greatest strength," Kamil says. "He is a kind humble man. He works hard for the money he brings home. And he loves you and your brothers and sisters."

Adel laughs. "Loves us? He doesn't see us! He does his own thing and only tells us to get out of his way."

Kamil shakes his head. "I don't know, but I can see that your father loves you in his own way. He is strict because he wants you and your brothers and sisters to grow up to be good people. I think he succeeded."

"No, it's because of my mother that we turned out to be good," Adel insists. "She is loving, kind and hard working. She's patient with my father and with all of us."

Kamil nods. "I completely agree with you, man. But you have to give some credit to your father."

Adel shakes his head. "I don't know. I just don't see it that way. I know you were there when we were growing up but you still can't understand how it is to be my father's son."

Kamil shrugs. "Well, maybe you never saw beyond yourself to see this. You always were able to get by with your good looks and charm."

Adel is surprised. "How can you say such things? I have nothing and it's all because of my father. I should have land, a house, a wife—but look at me!" Adel pauses. "Okay, forget about the wife part."

Kamil makes a face. "Yeah, sure, even if you did get all these things, you would have wanted more," he says. "You still would have left to come to the U.S. You told me that yourself. You want what you want and you get what you want."

Adel half laughs. "Wow, brother, I never thought you felt that way about me."

"Hey, I love you, man," Kamil replies, "but that means I gotta tell you the honest truth. So before you start thinking about going after Ms. Teacher, you better think about your wife first and try to work things out."

Adel sighs deeply. "You don't get it, Kamil. Even if Nora didn't come back in my life, there is no way that I'm going to stay with Yonka," he says. "She is the complete opposite of what I want in a wife."

Kamil nods. "Well, I'd have to say that you are right about that." Then he laughs again. "Man, if I saw my wife at home smoking pot with her co-workers, I think I'd divorce her on the spot!"

Adel laughs too. "I think if your wife was smoking pot in your home, she'd divorce herself on the spot." Both men laugh together at the thought.

Chapter 25

Nora and Michael

It is late in the evening and Nora and her fiancé Michael are having a heated discussion outside of Nora's townhouse.

Nora says to him, "You can't just take off every time we disagree on something."

"You know, I am just tired," Michael says, "and I have an early day tomorrow." He is a tall man with a receding hairline. He is dressed in an expensive suit— one of many in his collection. His hair, once the colour of hay, is now more silver than blonde. His eyes are a steel grey blue. His colleagues say his stare can hypnotize the most challenging dean or faculty member at the university in any meeting. The other female ESL teachers whisper to each other about why such a distinguished man like him would have any interest on the very young and naïve Nora.

Nora is upset. "Fine. Whatever." She turns and walks back towards her front door.

Michael follows her. "You know, if you weren't so moody maybe I wouldn't have to run away."

She whirls around. "Excuse me? What do you mean moody?"

He takes a deep breath. "For the past few weeks, you seem distracted and bothered. Everything I say, you've got something to say."

"Like what?" she asks.

"Like when I say, let's go look for at the new condos, you're always complaining that you're tired or another time."

She tries to calm down. "Well, I am tired. I've just got back to work and I've got so many lessons to prepare."

Michael shakes his head. "And I drive all the way out here which is a good forty minute drive just so that

I have to hear you bitch about all the work you have to prepare."

How insensitive he is! "Well, you know, since I got promoted to head teacher," she says, "I have to work extra hard to prove to everyone that I got the promotion because I deserve it. And not because I'm sleeping with my boss."

He half laughs. "You always have to blame it on that. I'm the director, not your manager. And I didn't give you the promotion so I don't know why you have to keep saying that."

Nora lowers her voice. "You don't understand. You don't hear the other teachers talking about me."

He says, "They're just jealous. Why let it bother you?"

I better tell him, she thinks to herself. "I was thinking of looking for a teaching job at another university."

Michael's eyes widen. "You know, when we get married, I was hoping you would just stop working."

"Oh, I see, and sit at home and do what?" She can't believe her ears.

"Be my wife! Mother to our kids."

She shakes her head. "You know, how romantic you make that sound?" she asks. "If you half meant it, maybe I would consider staying home and being your cook and nanny to *your* kids."

He turns away and starts heading to his car. "Okay, I'm going home now."

"See that's exactly what I mean," she says. "When we finally start talking, you run away."

He turns around. "You know, Nora, you're a pain and sometimes I wonder if it's worth the drive to come out here."

"I can count on my one hand how many times you drive out to see me in a month," she says. "I'm the one who always drives out to see you and I don't complain. It's because I look forward to seeing you so the drive is nothing to me. But you are always counting your pennies and worrying about how much you are spending on gas." Michael makes a face.

"And if you want to know the reason why I don't want to quit my job after we're married," she continues, "it is because I don't want to feel helpless and have you controlling me because you would have money and I wouldn't." There she finally told him the truth.

Michael walks towards his car without turning around. "See you at work tomorrow, Nora...good night."

He gets into his car and drives away. Nora watches him, tears streaming down her face.

Chapter 26

Lunch?

Weeks later at the school, the students are standing in the hall way lining up at the student activities table, excited about the upcoming Whistler weekend retreat. Nora is helping students sign up for the activity. Adel and Kamil are at the end of the line. Adel has been planning for this opportunity for days. He had done a little shopping on the weekend. He bought himself a new shirt and black pencil tight jeans. He had spent an hour in the morning combing and gelling his hair. And to top it off, he sprayed four big squirts of his favourite cologne "Eternity" by Calvin Klein. Yonka had made a face when she walked by him in the hallway that morning.

She greeted him with, "Did you just have a bath in a bottle of old cologne?"

When it was finally their turn to sign up for the retreat, Adel leans towards Nora. "I am looking forward to the retreat to Whistler this weekend."

Kamil leans forward and says, "Me too." Adel gives him a look.

He says to Nora, "I was happy to hear that we will be escorted by our instructors."

"Well, it won't all be fun and play," Nora says. "I do expect everyone to work on their projects at the retreat."

"Kamil and I are almost finished our project so that there will be more time for play." He winks at Kamil who laughs.

Nora can't help but smile. "Good day, Mr. Emre. I have another class soon and I need to get ready for them," she says.

Adel blurts out, "Are you free for lunch?"

Nora starts to say something. The bell rings for classes to start. The students disperse and head to their classrooms.

Nora looks around and then lowers her voice, "You know what? Sure... let's go for lunch."

Adel smiles widely. "I'll meet you here then?"

She bites her lip. "Actually, let's go off campus... I just don't want the other students and teachers to talk. Where are you parked?"

"In the parkade next door," he says.

"Okay, sure let's meet right outside." She quickly disappears around the corner towards her classroom.

Adel waves good-bye. When he turns around, he meets Kamil's stern frown.

"Don't you know she's engaged to the program director?" Kamil asks. "Would it be wise to be taking his fiancée out for lunch?"

Adel rolls his eyes. "Kamil, relax... You worry too much."

Kamil points his finger at him. "And don't forget that you are a married man."

Adel laughs. "Looks like you won't let me forget."

* * *

When the class is finished and her students start to leave, Nora quickly starts packing up her things. She looks up and is startled to see Michael standing by the door. He walks over to her desk.

"Want to go for lunch?" Michael asks. Nora takes a deep breath. Michael continues, "I have a meeting in forty-five minutes so let's get going."

Nora frowns. "Sorry, I have things to do. You go ahead."

He is surprised. "Okay, I'll see you later tonight then? Are you stopping by my place after work?"

Nora shakes her head. "Not tonight, Michael. I have to prepare for the Whistler retreat."

She quickly walks by him with her head down.

"Okay... call you later then?" he asks.

Nora keeps walking out the door leaving Michael standing alone in the classroom with a stunned expression on his face.

* * *

Nora steps outside the building. The cold wind blows her hair into her eyes. She zips up her jacket. Suddenly she feels unsure of herself. She hears the voices of her colleagues inside the building. Maybe he isn't going to show up after all. As she turns towards the parkade, she sees Adel leaning against the stair rail, smiling at her. She looks around to see if anyone is looking. She cautiously approaches him. His smile gets bigger the closer she steps towards him. When she climbs to the top step, he gives her his hand. She reaches out her hand but then hesitates.

"Mademoiselle," Adel says.

She checks over her shoulder, her heart pounding. What if the other teachers see her? She begins to doubt why she came. At that moment, the sound of Michael's voice fills her ears. "I want you to stay at home and be the mother to our kids."

She turns to Adel. "Monsieur Emre." They walk together into the parkade.

***

Adel speeds down the highway imagining his VW Golf is a sports car whipping around the race track in the Indy 500 and beside him is his Hollywood bride-to-be. He had purchased the car at the used car lot near Kamil's apartment just a few days ago. He believes that a man without a car is a man who cannot satisfy his woman.

"Whew... it feels like we're free from everything the farther we drive from campus." Nora giggles.

Adel smiles. "Freedom... yes, that is how I feel when I'm with you."

She laughs again. "Oh Adel... you are so funny."

"Why? It's the truth," Adel asks.

She shakes her head. "You just say exactly what you feel."

Adel says, "I don't know any other way."

He reaches out and puts his hand on top of hers. Nora attempts to pull away but then relaxes. They drive in silence for a few minutes.

Nora finally asks, "Where are you taking me?"

Adel shifts into third gear. "You'll see..."

After driving across the bridge into Richmond city, Nora becomes anxious wondering where he is taking her. Adel suddenly makes a turn and enters a quiet road. Nora notices a number of cars parked facing a chain link fence. Overhead she hears a loud rumbling sound and a large commercial airplane flies above them. Like a huge white eagle, the plane descends over the fence and touches down on to the tarmac in front of them. Adel looks over at Nora and squeezes her hand.

This was his surprise place he wanted to share with her weeks ago but had been too afraid to ask. He parks his car and then takes out the picnic basket—which he had prepared after Yonka left for work—from the back seat. "I reserved the best seats right up front."

Nora giggles. "How were you able to get tickets at such late notice?"

"I have a cousin that works at the ticket booth."

He takes out of the basket two turkey avocado sandwiches (which he made himself that morning), two bottles of cranberry juice (his favourite flavor), and two cups of pro-biotic strawberry yogurt (doesn't hurt to impress her with his awareness of healthy eating).

"How did you know I'd go to lunch with you?" she asks.

"Why you say this?" he replies.

"Well, you already had the picnic basket in your backseat so I'm assuming that you thought I would say yes to your invitation."

Adel laughs. "Well, how do you know I don't have an emergency basket of food in my car all the time?"

Her face turns red. "Oh yes. I didn't think about that."

He says, "Actually I was hoping you would come today but if you said no, I would be having a romantic picnic with Kamil right now."

They both laugh.

"Gosh, it's weird," Nora says, "for a moment I felt like we were back in LA at the airport watching the planes."

Adel nods his head in agreement. "It was one of the best moments in my life... and hopefully just the beginning of many more."

They search each other's eyes and slowly they move closer, lips almost touching. Then Nora stops and whispers, "I can't...I'm..."

Adel whispers back, "Shhhh..." and then the two kiss a sweet long kiss.

As they pull away, Adel says softly, "I've kissed women...and some were good kissers...but I cannot describe how I feel when I am kissing you."

Nora blushes. "I don't know if I should be jealous or flattered. Most guys I know would never admit anything so personal like that."

"It is how I feel and I want to share this with you," he says.

Nora nods. "Yes, I understand. I am just not used to it."

He strokes her face and kisses her forehead. He knows that if he continues, it would take them beyond what they were ready for. Usually he would be at the next step of romancing a woman which usually meant getting under the sheets. But Nora was different and he did not want to scare her away. He tells himself... be patient... she's worth waiting for.

Nora is relieved that Adel has not asked more from her. Logically she felt this was wrong but she wasn't sure if she would be able to stop herself if he asked.

Quietly, they both begin putting things back into the basket. He watches Nora out of the side of his eye.

On the drive back, she seems very distant in her thoughts as she looks out the window. Wordlessly, they both acknowledge that their brief moment together is now over and reality was waiting for them back at the university.

***

They arrive at the school and are walking outside the parkade. Nora takes out her business card, scribbles her number on the back and hands it to him.

"You'll remember to call this time?" she asks.

"Yes, I will," he replies. "Of course, unless I get deported." He grins.

Nora turns and lifts her hand to wave good-bye. "You can't use that same excuse this time, Mr. Emre."

.

Chapter 27

Stirring the pot

Yonka is sitting in her living room on the couch staring at an ultrasound photo of her baby—a girl. Having the image of her baby in her hand made her determined to protect this precious life inside of her. Mario, the real father of her child, was unaware that his unborn daughter was inside of her. How would her parents take the news? More importantly, how would her grandfather react? What about Mario's traditional Italian parents? No, staying in this arranged marriage was for the best, for herself and her unborn child.

She hears the front door open and Adel enters the room with his back pack on his shoulder. She tucks the photo into her purse.

Adel nods. "I'm glad you are home."

She raises her eyebrows. "Really?"

He drops his keys on the table. "We need to talk," he says.

She frowns as her heart skips a beat. Adel sits down unsure where to start. They sit in an awkward silence for some time. Finally, Adel clears his throat. "I think you probably know what I am going to say."

She stares at him. "No, I am not a mind reader."

He nods his head. "Well, this arrangement we have is not... not working," he says. "I think that it is best if we annul this while it is still early."

Yonka feels her face turn red. She fumbles with her words. "I don't understand. I thought we had an agreement. You live your life, I live mine and both our families will be happy."

Adel leans forward, elbows on his knees and looks down into his folded hands. "I know. It seemed to make sense at the time. But things have changed for me. I—I need to get on with my life. I can't live like this."

Yonka shakes her head, gets up and sits closer to him. "I still don't understand," she says. "This will devastate our family. "

"I'm sorry."

How could he do this to her? What was going on with him? "You can't do this," she insists. "Our families made an agreement. This is bigger than you or me."

He stands up annoyed now by her stubbornness. "There is no negotiation about this," he says. "I have made up my mind. I will look for a place and move out by the end of this month."

Yonka follows him down the hallway. She grabs his arm to stop him. "We can figure something out. If it's my smoking in the house, I can change that. I'll smoke outside on the balcony."

Adel refuses to look at her. "No, it's not that." He tries to walk past but Yonka steps in front of him.

"If it's smoking pot in the house, I won't do that anymore. I was planning to quit anyways. It's not good for the ba..." She stops herself.

"No, it's not that," he says. "It's not anything you can do." He walks around her and heads to his bedroom. His cell phone starts to ring. He checks and sees that it is Nora who is calling. His spirits begin to lift. He enters his room.

Yonka follows him and stops outside the doorway of his bedroom. "Adel, please." She has never begged for anything before.

He answers his cell phone and starts to close the door in Yonka's face. She pushes herself into the door frame to hold the door open.

Adel says into the phone, "Sorry, just a second." Then he gives Yonka a look and pushes the door firmly shut as Yonka steps back somewhat startled.

Yonka, not used to being refused or denied her wishes, is completely stunned. She stands there staring at the closed door. She hears Adel talking softly behind the door. She realizes that whomever he was speaking to was not Kamil. Was it a woman who called him? Who could this be? Was this why he wanted to annul their marriage? Devastated, she runs to her bedroom and slams the door shut. Angry tears stream down her face. She picks up the telephone and quickly dials Kamil's number. Kamil answers the phone.

"I need to talk with you," she snaps.

Startled, Kamil says, "Hello Yonka. What is this about?"

He glances over at his wife who is seated at the other end of the sofa, watching episode sixty of *"Fatmagülün Suçu Ne (What is Fatmagul's Fault?)"*. He half covers the phone. "I'm watching TV with Ayca right now."

Yonka barks, "I want to know who's the slut that Adel is seeing behind my back?"

Kamil's eyes widen and he coughs into his hand. "I don't know what you are talking about."

"Like hell you don't!" she yells. "You know everything about him. Tell me the truth!"

"Like I said, I don't know what you mean," he whispers into the phone. "I'm busy right now so I have to go."

Ayca looks up from the TV, not pleased. "Kamil, who is that on the phone?" she asks.

He reassures his wife. "It's Yonka… She thought Adel was with us. She's looking for him."

The last thing he needed tonight was Ayca nagging him about Adel again. The only way to keep her mouth shut was to make her happy and not to upset her. Keeping the peace in this house was difficult since his wife and his father-in-law had such volatile tempers. His wife was even more difficult to handle since she could easily go into a temper tantrum that could last for days and often ended with him on the living room sofa bed.

In a loud voice he says to Yonka, "If he comes by, I'll tell him to call you. Good night." He hangs up the phone while Yonka is in mid-sentence.

***

Her anger is now bubbling to the boiling point. Forget about Kamil, she thinks to herself. He's absolutely useless. She knows that the only person she can trust is her best friend Guy. He might have an answer for her. She quickly dials his number.

After a couple of rings, he answers, "Hey Yonka. What's up?"

"Adel is leaving me."

Unsurprised he says, "Why? What happened?" Here was Yonka again with one of her drama queen phone calls.

"Well, he says he wants to move on with his life. He wants to get an annulment."

Guy takes a sip from his latte which he was quietly enjoying before Yonka called. "And did he give you a reason?" he asks.

"Well, what do you think the reason would be?"

He replies, "He has a woman friend?" He pauses. "Or a guy friend?"

"Of course it's a *woman* friend," she snaps. She pauses and says, "Or that's what I am guessing."

"Guessing? Did he tell you he has a woman friend? Or are you just being paranoid?" He turns the page of his magazine, admiring the grey pin stripe pant suit the super thin model is wearing.

"He's in his room now talking to her on his cell phone with the door closed," she says. "Usually when he talks to anyone, he doesn't close his bedroom door."

"Well, what do you care?" he asks. "You are "seeing" Mario and having a long distance relationship with him." Yonka can be quite a hypocrite but that's what he loved about her. Spoiled rotten and wicked with a vulnerable side which she revealed only to him. He was her only confidante and he enjoyed being that for her.

"You don't understand," Yonka says. "It's not about that. It's about me being pregnant and the whole reason why I got into this whole arranged thing to begin with."

Guy frowns. "Sorry, I don't get it."

She continues in a hushed whisper. "I can't let my family find out that I got pregnant outside of marriage and to a non-Muslim man."

Guy nods his head slowly. "I see."

"I'm already three months pregnant," she says. "If he leaves me now before we actually consummate our marriage, my whole family will find out."

"Well, I doubt that he will be consummating with you anytime soon, dear," Guy says. "You're going to have to deal with it."

Yonka shakes her head and punches her hand into the pillow. "I can't "deal" with it!" she says. "My grandfather is the head of our family. He is the one who I run to when I need help financially. My parents are the same. If he finds out about this, he'll have me sent back to Turkey to live in the village with my distant cousins for the rest of my life."

Now this part of Yonka's culture was beyond him. The problems she encountered with her family seemed so backward. He says calmly, "But you are a grown woman. You have a fabulous career with a great salary. Why do you have to worry about your grandfather?"

"Because that is how it is. Unless I want him and my family to disown me, that is how things are." It sounded strange to her to hear the truth out in the open.

"So what are you going to do?" Guy asks. "Get Adel drunk and take advantage of him and then make him believe that he got you pregnant and live happily ever after?"

Suddenly a smile creeps onto Yonka's face as an idea pops into her head. "Thank you, Guy. You are a genius. I have to go," she says.

"Thank you for what?" he asks.

"I'll call you tomorrow," she says. "I really have to go."

Chapter 28

Nora makes some changes

Nora stands in her kitchen, her back to the living room as she whispers on her cell phone with Adel. Michael sits on the couch watching television. He turns to look at her, wondering who she is talking to. "Sorry, Michael dropped by unexpectedly," she says. "I can't really talk right now. "

"I understand," Adel says. "I have something that I need to say to you face to face anyway."

Nora frowns. "Is it something that I'm not going to like to hear, right?"

"Well, yes and no," he says.

Nora nods. "Okay so I'll talk to you later. Thanks for calling."

Adel can't help himself. "I'll dream of you tonight," he whispers.

She smiles. "Okay, that's enough."

"Really?" he asks.

She blushes. "No, I like it. It's nice."

He says, "It's the truth."

She smiles again. "Good night." She puts her phone down and walks into the living room.

Michael stands up. "Is everything okay?" he asks.

Nora walks up slowly towards him. Her hands are clammy and her throat tight. Suddenly, she feels like she is fifteen years old again. The self-confidence she had learned to embrace during her adulthood suddenly slithered away out the back door like a thief in the night. She takes a deep breath. "I'm glad that you're here. We need to talk."

Michael relaxes and smiles. "Is it wedding stuff? I'm afraid I'm not very good with organizing things like this. I was trusting that you would take care of everything."

She bites her lip nervously. "Actually, no... It's not about that."

His smile disappears. "I was hoping that it was something simple like that."

"Let's sit down," Nora says. She sits down on the couch. He sits beside her and loosens his tie.

She begins slowly. "I have been thinking a lot lately." A cold sweat covers her neck.

"Okay..." He frowns, unsure of where this is going.

Nora starts to stammer. "I think we have been rushing things a bit. I don't know if getting married in three months is the right thing to do."

Michael relaxes and sits back. "Well, is that all? Okay then, we can push the date to six months from now or twelve months. Whatever makes you feel good about it."

She can't believe that he was being so thick-headed. "Are you really ready to get married?"

Michael's eyebrows go up, shocked to hear this. After all, their wedding day was in a month. "Yes, of course I am. I wouldn't have asked you if I wasn't. Why would you ask me this? Don't you know me by now?"

"Well, that's just it. We have been together for a few years but I don't think I really do know you." She pauses knowing he will start in on her with his usual rant.

Michael shakes his head. "Here we go again..." He stands up and begins pacing slowly back and forth in front of her. Watching him was almost hypnotic. "Sure you know me. We've been together on and off since I was your prof in university. I don't know what you don't know about me."

He stops and sits down abruptly turning to her. "The problem isn't what you don't know; it's what you won't accept."

He grabs Nora's hand, squeezing it tightly. "I am who I am," he says. "I'm not a knight in shining armor ready to take you off on my white horse. I'm not this romantic ideal man you've dreamed about since you were a little girl. Trust me... There's no such thing."

Nora's face turns red with fury.

"What I am is a man who will be committed to working with you to make a family and home together. I will make sure that you get the things you need. And I will not give up on us."

She blurts out, "You're right. You're absolutely right. It's not you... It's me. You have never pretended to be something you are not. You definitely are not the romantic but hey I knew that going in. The problem is... Is it enough?"

Michael rolls his eyes. "What do you want Nora? This is the real world we're living in. This isn't a romance novel or a movie. Men and women who are compatible with each other and who care about each other is what makes a good marriage."

She says, "Logically, yes I agree, but..."

"But what?" Michael shouts unable to control his anger.

"I need time to think about things," she says. "I think we got back together without resolving any of the issues before we broke up." Her last words sound more like a shrill cry of despair. Whatever shred of composure she had, disappeared as it always did when she was with him.

Michael reaches out and pulls her close to him. He holds her chin up and looks into her eyes.

He says reassuringly, "It's normal to get cold feet before the wedding day."

Repulsed, she pulls herself out of his embrace. She turns away from him in disbelief.

He continues unperturbed. "Hey, sometimes I get that feeling too. But then I brush it away because I know deep in my heart that you are the one for me."

The tears she promised not to cry, start burning her cheeks.

"I know you feel the same way," he says. "I don't think that I need to give you flowers every day and recite poetry to you to convince you that I mean it when I say, I want to be with you. So if you want to take a short break to think. Sure, go ahead. I'll leave you alone for two weeks if that helps. Then we can talk again. How's that?"

Nora nods slowly almost robotically. It was like reliving their last "break up" all over again. She says, "Okay. Maybe you're right. Thank you for understanding what I'm going through."

He smiles now relieved that his little Nora was back to her old self. He gives her a big hug. "Okay, so I'll let you be alone so that you can figure stuff out. We'll talk again exactly two weeks from now. Okay?"

She tries to smile. "Okay. Thanks."

He gets up quickly, picks up his jacket and heads to the door. His mission is *fait accompli*, mission accomplished.

Nora slowly follows behind him. He turns around, leans over and gives her an obligatory kiss on the cheek as if nothing had happened. He opens the front door and walks to his black shiny BMW sport utility vehicle without looking back. She closes the door behind him. Her mind is numb with frustration and self-disgust. Why did she let him do this to her again?

Chapter 29

Never underestimate Yonka

Back home, Kamil watches Adel packing his sport bag. He is getting ready for the Whistler retreat. Kamil had packed his bag the night before—he wasn't one to wait till the last minute. He was excited to be getting out of the house this weekend. His life at his wife's parents' home was always tense. He never felt at home there. His wife who is so insecure and over-protective literally is smothering the life out of him.

"If you weren't going on the retreat, Ayca would never let me go," he says.

Adel smiles. "Glad to be of usefulness to you."

"Lucky you and I don't have to share our room with Kenko," Kamil says. "He thinks he's so smart just because he has a rich dad and he drives a Mercedes."

Adel laughs. "You're just jealous."

Kamil shakes his head. "No...I'm not." They both laugh. It is just like old times before their arranged marriages. Life was so much simpler then.

There is a soft knock on the door. Kamil looks at Adel who raises his eyebrow. The door opens and Yonka enters, dressed in a respectable grey dress. Who is this standing before them? Her face has only a little bit of makeup unlike her usual "fashionista" diva face paint she puts on every morning. Her hair is tied back neatly. She almost resembles a respectable woman, Adel thinks to himself. Something fishy was going on.

"I made dinner. I was wondering if both of you would like to join me?" she says softly.

Adel starts to say, "Well, I'm getting ready for the retreat..."

Kamil jumps up from the bed. He walks by Adel, pulling his elbow. "Mmmm... it smells wonderful. We'd love to join you."

Yonka smiles. "Great. I made Izmir köfte. It's my mother's favourite dish."

Kamil rubs his hands in anticipation. "We haven't had that in a long time. Right, Adel?" Adel nods and reluctantly follows them to the dining room.

Adel and Kamil are shocked to see the feast that is laid out before them. The table is set with a white table cloth, matching white plates, wine glasses and candles. A large white serving dish with köfte is in the centre. Appetizers of dolmari, humus, olives, baby dill pickles, and Turkish salad surround the main dish.

Adel, his mouth open, is in complete disbelief. Yonka never made a meal for him before. The only food he ever saw her prepare was her Weight Watchers frozen entrées. Kamil is smiling widely—obviously impressed. He pulls out a chair and quickly starts serving himself.

Yonka smiles demurely showing her pleasure at their reaction. Adel sits at the head of the table and looks at all the food in front of him.

Yonka sits to his left. "What would you like to start with?" Adel is silent. She smiles and starts to scoop köfte onto his plate.

"Wow, I didn't know that you are a good cook," Kamil says. "I thought Ayca is good but this is amazing."

Yonka blushes. "Being the only girl, my mother made sure that I learned how to cook and prepare meals for my father."

Adel still not convinced, says, "Why haven't you cooked like this before?"

"I hated having to prepare meals all day for my father and brothers," Yonka says. "When I left home, I didn't want to be reminded of those days so I stopped making these dishes."

Adel, skeptical that his spoiled brat cousin was suddenly thinking about someone other than herself, says, "So what makes you want to make it now?"

Kamil gives Adel a dirty look. Why can't he just relax and enjoy the moment? Why does he always think the worse of his cousins?

"Well, since you said you are planning to move out in a few weeks," Yonka says, "I thought that we could enjoy a traditional Turkish meal together. The three of us. We are family after all."

Adel is not convinced. Before he can open his mouth to ruin the evening, Kamil says, "Well, thank you very much. You should open a Turkish restaurant. I'm sure you would get many customers."

Yonka laughs. "I guess I have that to fall back on. But I don't have any interest in running a business."

Adel takes a bite. He is absolutely shocked. The food was more than delicious—it was even better than how his mother makes köfte—which of course he would never admit out loud to anyone. A mother's cooking is sacred and never open to any disrespect under any circumstance. He takes another huge bite and nods his head in pleasure.

He says, "Kamil is right. You could open a restaurant. The food is very delicious. And you work in the hotel industry. You know the tourism, food and hospitality industry."

She smiles slyly. "I would need your business sense to make it a success."

Adel smiles at her, pleased with the compliment. "Well, I do enjoy running my own business."

Kamil, glad to see that Adel and his wife are finally getting along, says, "He is a natural business man. Did he tell you when we were in LA, we came with nothing and within months, Adel was running his own shuttle business that was better than my cousin who has been running his business for years?"

Yonka turns to Adel. "Wow, that is impressive."

Adel smiles proudly. "Well, it took a lot of hard work. It wasn't easy," he says.

She pours *raki*, a traditional Turkish alcoholic drink, into their glasses.

"No, no, thank you," Adel says. "We shouldn't. We have to get up early for tomorrow."

"Come on, Adel," Kamil says. "This is not just any drink... This is raki. When do we get to eat a good meal with a traditional Turkish drink?" He reaches for the bottle and pours more in his glass and fills Adel's to the top.

Adel nods his head. "You're right, Kamil," he says. "Good food, good drink." He first takes a sip, smiles and then takes a big gulp.

It was a surreal evening with the three of them, enjoying each other's company—eating, laughing, and drinking together like a real family. Adel wonders if they had more moments like this, maybe things could have been better. Maybe being married to Yonka wouldn't be such a bad thing?

***

At the end of the evening, after sitting in the living room and chatting, Kamil tells Adel and Yonka that he should head home. Ayca had already called his cell phone three times asking why he was not home yet. He gets up to leave. Adel stands up to walk him to the door. Kamil looks over at Yonka who is politely sitting on the couch like a traditional wife.

"Good night. Yonka," he says. "That was a delicious meal. Thank you again." He tells Adel, "Pick me up at seven thirty in the morning, okay?"

Adel says, "Sure. Good night." He closes the door behind him. It was a good night but he really needed to get to bed. The retreat was tomorrow and he didn't want to miss the chartered bus in the morning.

"Thanks again for tonight," he says to Yonka. "I think I will go to sleep now. I have a long day tomorrow." He smiles at her and then turns to go to his room.

"One more drink before bed?" Yonka asks.

Adel looks at her and half smiles. "No, really I have to get up early tomorrow for the trip to Whistler."

"Ahh... the retreat," she says. She walks by him towards the kitchen.

"How about some Turkish coffee? Come on. I saved some baklava for us. Why not end the night with a hot drink and dessert?"

She walks into the kitchen. Adel pauses for a second and then follows her. Turkish coffee and baklava—who could resist?

Yonka pours the coffee into large mugs. Adel is a bit surprised. Traditional Turkish coffee is usually served in very small coffee cups. Yonka gives him a knowing smile and brings out a bottle of Baileys Irish whiskey. Adel shakes his head and gives her a funny smile.

Yonka says slyly, "I heard Kamil say that this is your favourite evening treat when you were in the States. Spanish coffee with a bit of Bailey's liqueur."

"Well, well, well," Adel says. "I don't know what you are up to."

Yonka gives him a puzzled look. "I do not know what you mean?" she asks. "Can't I make at least one day as your wife something worth remembering?"

He half chuckles to himself. "You know, Yonka, I think us not being husband and wife is a good thing," he says. "See how much better we are getting along since we decided to end this?"

She snaps. "You mean since *you* decided to end this." She regains her composure. "But let's not be petty."

She pours the liqueur into their mugs. "Could you be a good husband and get some whipped cream from the freezer?"

Adel nods his head and goes to the fridge. With her back to him, she quickly pulls out a small vial and pours the white powdery contents into Adel's mug.

Adel, unknowingly, searches the freezer, looking for the tub of Cool Whip which she usually keeps for her late night pie cravings. He cannot seem to find it. "Are you sure it's in here? I can't see it."

Yonka picks up her mug and takes a sip. "Actually, I think I forgot that we ran out last week."

Adel straightens up. "That's okay. Milk should be enough."

Yonka pours the milk into his mug and stirs it. She looks up at him and hands him the drink.

He sips it, nods his head. "Ahh... thank you, Yonka. This is a good way to end the night."

She smiles and hands him a few pieces of baklava on a small plate. He picks one up and takes a bite. The sweetness pours into his mouth like sugary gold. He takes another sip of coffee.

"There are a lot of left-overs," she says. "Would you like me to pack you a lunch?"

He thinks about it. Why not? The meal she made was probably better than the fast food they would be eating up at the retreat. "Sure, Kamil would really like that," he says. "I'm sure that food is quite expensive up at Whistler."

Yonka nods. "Oh yes... I remember the last time I was there. I was shocked that one avocado costs five dollars."

Adel is shocked. "Is that true?"

Yonka nods.

"That is criminal!" he says. "How can they markup fruit 400%?"

"Well it's a tourist town," she replies, "and that's what they do. There's nowhere else for you to buy stuff unless you drive a half hour away from Whistler Village."

He says, "Ah, and we are going by bus so I won't be able to drive anywhere."

"See what I mean?" she says.

Adel puts his cup down and suddenly the room begins to spin around him.

Yonka watches him carefully. "Oh my gosh, Adel, are you okay?"

The ground seems to sway beneath his feet. He tries to balance himself. "I don't know... I am not feeling well." He holds the counter for support.

Yonka slides up to him and puts his arm on her shoulder. "Maybe you need to lie down. Let me help you."

Adel stumbles as Yonka tries to hold him up. She leads him down the hall.

"I am so dizzy. The room is spinning," he mumbles.

Yonka opens the door to her room. "Don't worry. You'll feel better if you lie down."

He moans, shaking his head from left to right. Yonka helps him down on the bed. She disappears to the bathroom for a few minutes. She returns with a damp face towel. Adel tries to sit up. She firmly pushes him back onto the pillow and wipes his forehead.

"Shhhh.... just relax and sleep. You'll be fine."

Adel mutters, "I - I- don't..."

Yonka whispers into his ear, "Just relax..."

Adel stops struggling and drifts into a restless sleep.

* * *

Convinced that Adel had finally fallen asleep, Yonka gets up from the bed. She lets her hair out of the pony tail and slips off her dress to reveal the lacy red lingerie underneath. She sits beside Adel and removes his shirt. He tries to push her away but his arms are limp.

She pulls down his pants and tosses them on the floor. When she turns back she notices that he is wearing a Turkish brand of underwear, Hike Sport, a knock-off of the popular Nike brand. She wonders how his lady friend reacted when she saw him in them. Was she polite or did she laugh in his face?

She reaches down and removes his socks, careful to use only two fingers. She makes a face as she tosses them on the floor. She reaches for her cell phone on the night stand. She holds the phone up with the camera pointed at herself and Adel. Still holding the camera up, she puts her face close to him and kisses him on the cheek. She takes a picture to capture the moment. Next, she turns his face to hers, posing seductively while taking a few more pictures. Later she reviews the photos on her cell phone. She smiles to herself, pleased that the photos turned out perfectly. Anyone looking at them would be convinced the man and woman in the pictures were sharing an extremely intimate moment together.

Chapter 30

What just happened?

Early the next morning, Adel is awakened by the beeping of the alarm on his watch. He slowly opens his eyes. He tries to lift his head but the pounding between his ears forces him to lay back. Suddenly a golden tanned arm reaches over and hugs him. Startled, he looks down and sees Yonka's head on his shoulder. He tries to recall what happened earlier but his memory fails him. Adel gently lifts Yonka's head off his shoulder so as not to wake her. Only then does he notice that much of her body is exposed, the lace only hiding the most private parts. She must sunbathe in the nude, he thinks to himself.

He glances down to see that he only has his underwear on. He stumbles out of the bed, looks around and realizes he is in Yonka's room. He turns to look for the rest of his clothes and in doing so trips over his shoes. On the ground, on all fours, he spots his jeans, his shirt and socks and hastily picks them up from the floor. Yonka grunts and turns over in the bed. Adel scrambles to the door with his clothes in his hands.

Yonka opens her eyes to see Adel fumbling with the door knob. "Honey?" She uses the term of endearment knowing it would freak him out even more.

Adel glances back for a second before he flings the door open and races out of the room.

***

On the bus ride to the retreat, Adel stares out the window, oblivious of the students around him.

"What's wrong Adel?" Kamil asks. "I am talking as if I am by myself. Is everything okay?"

Adel shakes his head and looks out the window—the coastline blurred by his thoughts. He mumbles, "Nothing... It's nothing."

Kamil looks down the aisle and sees Nora. She is dressed in a cashmere pink sweater and black jeans which made her blend in with the rest of the students. It was a side of his teacher that he had never seen before since she only wore professional suits at the university. He felt that maybe he could be friendlier with her. She flashes him a warm smile. Kamil cannot resist. "Come sit down here, Ms. Morgan."

Nora waves but shakes her head politely.

He laughs and turns to Adel. "Well, I tried."

Adel is silent. Kamil shrugs his shoulders. "What is the matter? Did you and Yonka fight again last night? I thought we were having such a pleasant evening together. "

Adel's face turns red. "Yonka... she planned all this. She... she set me up."

Kamil frowns. "What are you talking about? You sound like you have had one glass too many of raki."

Adel talks to himself. "I should have known. I should have known. She tricked me..." He clenches his hand and hits his fist on his thigh.

Kamil looks around, worried that the other students were listening. "Adel, tell me what you are talking about," he says. "You are really beginning to scare me."

Adel lowers his voice. "Last night, something happened."

Kamil's eye brow goes up. "Huh?"

"I don't know," Adel says. "I can't remember... I know that after you left she made some Spanish coffees."

Kamil smirks. "And both of you did a little romance..."

Adel grimaces. "No, we were just talking in the kitchen," he says. "That's it... and then I remember feeling like the room was spinning. And later, I became weak."

"Sounding like you got drunk, man," he says.

Adel pauses but then shakes his head. "No, I wasn't drunk. I can't get drunk from Spanish coffee. And I was fine before that."

"Okay, so what happened?"

"I don't know," Adel says. "Really... I cannot remember. I woke up this morning and... "

This was getting exciting. Kamil nods his head, encouraging his friend to continue.

"I didn't know where I was," Adel continues, "and.. and.. I look down and see Yonka is sleeping beside me."

Kamil bursts out laughing. "What? Are you joking me?"

Adel puts his hand on Kamil's mouth. "Shhh. Lower your voice..."

Kamil nods, motioning for him to continue. Adel removes his hand from his mouth. Kamil starts to say something but Adel points a finger at him in warning. Kamil presses his lips together to show Adel that he was going to behave.

Adel takes a deep breath. "I wake up and think that I'm having a bad dream...and then I close my eyes to see if I can wake myself from the nightmare. When I open my eyes, she is still beside me. I look around and I'm not in my room. I'm in *her* room!"

Kamil's eyes widen. "Oh wow."

Adel continues. "I didn't know what to do but grab my clothes and run out of there."

Kamil interrupts. "What do you mean *grab your clothes*?"

Adel shakes his head.

Kamil begins to piece the events together. "So you two...?"

Adel shakes his head again. "No... No... I don't ... I don't think. No. No..."

Kamil continues. "You are in her room, in her bed, out of your clothes... and she is wearing... or not wearing...?"

Adel moans. "I didn't really look but..."

"But what?" Kamil cannot wait to hear Adel's explanation.

Adel says quietly, "She is wearing something."

"Ah, come on," Kamil says. "Something? What something?"

Adel mumbles, "Something for sleeping."

Kamil laughs. "You mean like sexy something?"

Adel nods his head.

"So you two finally had your honeymoon."

Adel looks up from his hand. "No! We did not! She... she set me up."

Kamil makes a face. "What are you talking about?" he asks. "Did it ever occur to you that maybe you two were enjoying each other's company and then one thing led to another?"

"No! No! That's not what happened."

Kamil asks, "What do you mean? You think she *forced* you to go to her room and sleep with her?"

"Yes... she did." The words leave Adel's lips like the air leaking from a flat tire.

Kamil bursts out laughing. "Please explain, dear friend, how she did that?"

"I think she put something in my coffee," Adel says. "I got sick and dizzy after drinking... Yes... yes, that's what happened. And then she helped me to her room and I must have passed out."

Kamil shakes his head in disbelief.

Adel nods his head. "Yes, that's when she must have taken my clothes off and then made it look like we slept together."

Kamil rolls his eyes. "Or... you had a lot of raki during dinner and then some rum in your coffee. Then you two had a good time but you were too drunk to remember in the morning."

Adel shakes his head. "No, no, no. We didn't do anything."

Kamil takes a deep breath. "So maybe what you say is true. Are you absolutely, positively sure that *nothing* happened after you were in her bed?"

Adel bites his lip. He closes his eyes trying to recall if anything physical did happen.

Finally, he says, "I am pretty sure... but... not positive." He puts his head in his hands.

Kamil lowers his voice. "You know you won't be able to get your annulment if you both consummated the marriage."

Adel's face turns red. "And that's how Yonka figured out how to get what she wants. She doesn't want us to get an annulment. That bitch." He punches his leg in disgust.

Chapter 31

Whistler, British Columbia

After what seemed the longest ride of Adel's life, the bus finally arrives at the Whistler Lodge. Adel and Kamil quickly check in at the hotel counter and then proceed up to their suite. Their classmate Zeid catches up to them announcing that he is the lucky student who will also be sharing their suite. When they enter, there is a large couch and a smaller couch and a chair in the living area. The check-in clerk had told them that there was a sofa bed in their suite.

Zeid, being this was his first time away from his parents, excitedly asks, "Who's sleeping on the sofa bed?"

Adel and Kamil give each other a look.

Kamil smiles widely. "Since you asked for it first, it's all yours."

Adel nods his head and brings his bag to one of the bedrooms. "Yes, yes, I agree. I won't fight over it."

Kamil brings his bag to the other bedroom and waves good-bye to Zeid.

After a second, Zeid raises his eyebrow. "Hey, wait a minute...." He scratches his head. He realizes that he lost out on claiming a bedroom for himself. He shrugs. He is happy all the same. He puts his bag on the chair and starts taking out his things.

Kamil calls out. "Don't forget, guys! We have to be in the lobby in one hour for lunch."

***

Lunch was buffet style at the hotel's restaurant. Adel, Kamil and Zeid enjoyed piling the food onto their plates and going back for seconds. Once lunch is over, the first class activity begins. Nora and three other teachers lead the groups through the Whistler village. Adel is walking with his head down, hands in his pockets. Kamil is walking close by but is chatting with Zeid and two other classmates. Nora is walking with Ms. Myrtle and another teacher. She can see out of the corner of her eye that Adel is not his usual self. She tries to catch his attention but with little luck. Kamil catches her eye and gives her a reassuring smile. She nods her head in acknowledgement.

Later in the day, the teachers bring the students in groups of five to the gondola ride. The students are asked to describe the scenery as they ride up the mountain. Kamil is overwhelmed by the view of the mountain side, the trees and how high above the ground they were. Nora asks each student to describe what they see out the window. Zeid takes advantage of the opportunity to be the first to describe the view as this would surely impress Ms. Morgan. After he finishes, Nora pats him on the arm and tells the other students to follow his lead. Zeid is pleased with himself.

Adel looks out the window, his mind elsewhere. Kamil shakes his head and sighs. When it is his turn, Kamil blurts out, "Never have I seen such wondrous beauty and grandeur. This moment with you and I together here is remarkable and forever memorable." The class giggles and Nora blushes.

"Thank you for that wonderful and colourful description, Kamil."

She turns to Adel, "And Adel, how would you describe what you see outside the window?"

Adel is still staring out the window. He is unaware that all the students are waiting for his response.

Nora is losing her patience. "Mr. Emre, did you hear me?"

Adel looks up at her and then to the other students. Kamil tries to mouth to him what the question is.

"It seems that you have something on your mind today," Nora says. "But I need to remind you that this is a class activity and not just a free day."

Adel tries to smile but can't. He finally manages to say, "Yes, Ms. Morgan."

Nora clears her throat. "I'll see you after lunch to discuss this further." Adel nods his head.

"Let's continue, everyone." Nora turns back to the other students and continues with the activity.

Kamil whispers to Adel, "Come on, don't let Yonka ruin the trip for all of us."

Adel nods his head. "Okay, I'll try."

* * *

Later that evening, the class returns to the hotel and gathers in the lobby foyer.

A teacher, Ms. Suarez, prepares an announcement. "The rest of the day is free but we do ask that everyone please be down here at seven thirty a.m. sharp tomorrow so that we can have breakfast on time. Skiing lessons are at twelve noon tomorrow so we don't want to be late for that."

A few students clap and excitedly nod their heads when hearing the word *skiing*.

Nora walks close to Adel. "Can we talk now about your participation today ... or lack of?"

Adel looks at Nora. "Yes, Ms. Morgan."

Nora says quietly, "Meet you at the Starbucks across the street."

She walks out the front doors. Kamil looks over at Adel who gives him a nod. Before he can say anything, Adel walks through the doors after her.

When Adel enters the Starbucks, he sees Nora at the counter ordering a coffee. He walks to the end of the line. She turns, sees him and motions for him to come up to the front. He smiles and moves up beside her.

"What would you like?" she asks.

"My usual, Ms. Morgan."

Nora smiles and turns to the cashier. "Tall, black."

The cashier calls back to the worker. "One tall, black."

Adel is pleased that she had remembered how he liked his coffee.

They stand in silence waiting for their drinks. When they are ready, Adel and Nora decide to walk outside.

Nora starts the conversation. "I hope everything is okay. You seemed so distant today."

Adel sighs. "Can we find somewhere warm? I think we need to sit and talk."

Nora says, "We can go back to the hotel. "

Adel shakes his head. "Can't... Too many eyes."

"We can meet in my room."

Adel is shocked. He looks at her.

Nora says, "Hey... just to talk... nothing like that. Don't get the wrong idea."

Adel turns to her. "I would never think that way. You know that." He touches her hand. She smiles.

She says, "Room 324." He nods and walks ahead.

***

When Adel enters his hotel room, Kamil, Zeid and two other classmates, Masahiro and Miguel, are playing poker.

"Hey Adel," Miguel says. "What take you so long, man? We deal you in next hand."

"Oh, hey guys," Adel says.

Masahiro comes up to him and attempts to give Adel a *high five* handshake as Kamil had taught him earlier but fails miserably. Everyone laughs, including Adel who is beginning to loosen up.

Masahiro says, "Did Ms. Morgan kick you ass? Haha."

Adel coughs in his hand. He replies, "Oh yeah... She's a tough teacher."

Kamil pulls back a chair for him to sit.

Adel says, "Let me get changed first. I'll be back in a bit." They nod their heads and continue with their game.

Zeid says, "Hurry up, roommate. I need to make my money back from you."

Kamil chuckles.

Adel goes into his room and shuts the door. He dials Nora's cell phone.

After a few rings, she answers. "Hello Adel."

"Is it okay if I come by in an hour instead? There is a poker party happening in my room."

Nora smiles. "I understand. Sure. The other teachers called me to come down for a swim. If you feel like joining us after your game, I'll see you down there. If not, call me later."

Adel whispers, "Oh.. why you torture me like this? I'll lose my shoes thinking of you in your swimming suit."

Nora giggles. "You mean your underwear."

Adel says, "Huh?" Nora says, "The proper idiom is *lose my underwear*."

Adel laughs. "And that too."

Now they both are giggling. This was an inside joke among the class. Nora had a homework assignment where the students had to write an essay using Canadian idioms. Masahiro had read his essay to the class and said that "I lost my underwear thinking about this homework assignment." The class had burst out laughing.

Adel says, "I will lose as fast as I can and join you at the pool."

"You are funny, Adel."

"No, I'm telling you the truth," he says.

"See you soon. Bye," she says. Adel hangs up the phone. His spirits have definitely picked up. Yes, he should take Kamil's advice and not let Yonka ruin his trip.

Chapter 32

Rest and relaxation

Adel holds two aces in his hand. There is an Ace on the flop and two Kings on the turn. Miguel, a regular poker player at the local casinos, confidently raises twenty dollars. He was confident that he would empty all the wallets of the other players tonight. Kamil and Masahiro fold. Adel re-raises another twenty dollars. Zeid, seeing that the stakes are going up in the double digits, folds his hand. Miguel, not swayed, calls Adel's hand. Masahiro deals the river card which is an Ace. Miguel quickly raises his hand. Everyone watches

Adel who hesitates. Suddenly, he pushes his chips and says "All in." He has put in all the money he brought for the trip which was just over two hundred dollars.

Kamil looks at him nervously. The pot is now over three hundred dollars. The amount of money on the table was almost half of Kamil's wages at his father-in-law's restaurant.

Miguel gives Adel a look. "Adel, I'm not sure if you have something in your hand or if you are big bluffer or if you have the real deal. You have such a good poker face." Had it been a scene in a James Bond movie, the moment might have been quite suspenseful. In this case, due to the stress, Miguel's Filipino accent became stronger with the sound of the letter "f" turning into the letter "p" and vice versa. So the last two words from his mouth come out as "foker pace" which make Kamil and Zeid burst out into laughter. Being ESL (*English as a second language*) students, they often made fun of each other's accents.

Adel looks Miguel calmly in the eye. "Come on, Miguel. Are you in or not?"

Miguel says, "Oh yeah..I'm in." He pushes his stacks of chips in.

"Okay show your cards," Masahiro says.

Miguel puts down his cards, revealing an Ace and a King. He has a full house—which to him was an excellent hand. He says to Adel, "Give me my money, paré." (*Paré* means *friend* in Tagalog.) He reaches for the pile of chips.

Adel smiles from ear to ear. "Wait a minute, paré." He throws down his cards. "I've got four aces!"

The other guys start laughing and howling, seeing that Adel's four-of-a-kind beats Miguel's full house by a long shot. Four Aces was definitely overkill. Adel smiles from ear to ear. He pulls the pile of chips towards him. He was three hundred dollars richer and enjoying every minute of it. Miguel shakes his head and hits his hand on the table. He says a swear word in Filipino and gets up and takes out a cigarette.

"Okay, you got me. I'm going out for a smoke." He steps out on the balcony.

"Hey, hey, you cannot smoke on the balcony," Kamil says and points to the sign on the wall.

Miguel makes a face. "I'm going downstairs then for 10 minutes. But then we get back to the game." He points to Adel, "I want to get my money back."

Adel shakes his head. "Sorry, I've got plans."

Everyone looks at him. Kamil asks, "What plans?"

"I'm going to the pool," he says. Adel gets up and goes to his room.

"Well, we should all go for a swim," Zeid says. Everyone agrees.

Kamil says, "But you don't have your swimming suit."

Zeid laughs. "Well, we can go Turkish style, right?" Everyone laughs too.

While everyone is getting ready, Adel rifles through his bag and digs out his black speedo and a towel. He is ready for some action.

***

Lounging around the hot tub, Nora and two other teachers are catching up with the latest gossip. Nora, dressed in a classic blue one piece bathing suit, Ms. Suarez, in an Olympic style one piece, and Ms. Myrtle, in a hot red bikini— the teachers have the attention of all the students in the pool. Kamil, Zeid and Miguel come out of the showers and head towards the other students. A couple of girls call out asking if they would sit with them. Kamil and Zeid's mouth drop when they see their teachers sitting around the hot tub in their lounge chairs.

Suddenly the pool becomes silent when one of the girls calls out, "There's Adel!"

Adel strides out of the shower room confidently. He is lean and muscular and proudly wearing his black speedo. Nora looks up at him, her eyes widening. The other teachers also stare. Kamil and the other male students are in complete awe. Adel nods at Nora with a little smile and walks over to the deep end of the pool. The girls in the pool are frozen, their eyes following Adel's every move. Miguel and the other guys start elbowing one another, giggling and laughing. Adel, unaware of the commotion, calmly walks onto the diving board. He runs and does a perfect dive into the water. The girls squeal with delight and begin pointing at him.

"Ah, come on," Miguel says. He is annoyed at all the attention he wasn't getting from them. Zeid shakes his head while Kamil smiles to himself.

Adel starts to swim like an Olympic medalist going for the gold with perfect butterfly strokes. He swims towards the end of the pool where the other students are.

"Let's get out of here," Miguel calls out to the other guys. "This is lame." The girls "ooh" and "ahhh" as Adel swims closer to them.

Miguel, Zeid and the male students start climbing out of the pool. They are all dressed in long surfer shorts. They look at Adel with disgust. Adel reaches the end and he pulls himself up out of the pool. He looks towards the hot tub and gives his teachers a disarming smile. Nora giggles to herself while Ms. Myrtle starts some of her own "oohing" and "ahhing".

Miguel says, "Nice speedo, Adel!" Zeid and the other boys start to snicker. Adel turns to look at them. He then realizes that he is the only one wearing a speedo. Even Kamil was wearing shorts.

"Nice dive, Adel," Lucy, the Korean student nods her head in approval. "You're such a good swimmer!" another one chirps. The girls start giggling and teasing him.

Adel gives them a nod and then walks straight for the hot tub. He climbs into the hot tub, smiles at his teachers. He proceeds to find a seat between Nora and Ms. Myrtle. Ms. Myrtle moves over to give him space to sit.

"Well Adel, that was very impressive," says Ms. Suarez, nodding her head in appreciation.

"Yes, you obviously are very comfortable in the water," Ms. Myrtle says in a flirty voice.

Nora is giggling into her hand. "That was a beautiful dive."

Adel blushes. "Growing up in a fishing town, everybody knows how to swim before they learn how to walk."

Nora gives him a big smile.

Ms. Myrtle says, "Well, you know it's refreshing to see someone wearing proper swimming attire. Most Canadian men don't have the courage to wear a speedo these days."

Ms. Suarez elbows Ms. Myrtle in the ribs. Nora giggles again. Adel notices Nora's hand near him and he reaches out to hold it. She pulls her hand away.

The boys from the pool are snickering after hearing Ms. Myrtle's comments.

"Aw, shut up... She's right you know," Lucy says to them.

Miguel and Zeid give Lucy and her friends dirty looks and jump back into the pool. This Adel sure took the fun out of their swimming party.

"This is what we wear to swim," Adel says. "I can't imagine wearing pants in the pool." He flashes his teachers a charming smile.

Ms. Myrtle is smitten and perhaps a little drunk. She had started cocktail hour a little earlier than usual that day. She comes up close to Adel and puts her hand on his knee.

"You are so European," she says in a husky whisper. "I really like Europe you know..."

Ms. Suarez pulls Ms. Myrtle back. "Okay Nancy. I think you've had just a little too many margaritas tonight. Let's get you upstairs."

Ms. Myrtle shakes her away and comes up close to Adel. "Say Adel... could you teach me how to dive? I've always wanted to learn."

Ms. Suarez stands up and pulls Ms. Myrtle up. "Nancy, let's go."

Ms. Myrtle pouts. "But..."

Ms. Suarez says, "No buts... let's go."

Nora stands up. "I'll help you bring her upstairs."

Ms. Suarez shakes her head. "No, that's okay. You just got here. Enjoy yourself for a little while longer. Plus we need to have a teacher here with the students before they close the pool in twenty minutes."

Nora looks over at the clock. "Oh, okay. See you tomorrow morning then. Good luck with Ms. Myrtle."

Ms. Myrtle frowns as she struggles to climb out of the hot tub. "What do you mean good luck?" She turns to Adel. "I'd love to have you in my class, sweetie."

Ms. Suarez says, "Come on..." and pulls her out of the hot tub and heads her straight into the ladies shower room.

Nora turns to Adel. He smiles again. "Well, Ms. Morgan, I best join the other students." He whispers into her ear, "You look absolutely beautiful by the way. I'll meet you in your room in thirty minutes."

Nora blushes and nods. She didn't realize what a *Casanova* Adel was. Adel climbs out of the hot tub starting another round of squeals from the girls. He walks over to the end of the pool and joins the girls. They surround him like sharks giggling, laughing and flirting.

Miguel says to the guys, "Let's play poker. This scene is lame." Zeid and the other guys agree and climb out of the pool. Kamil climbs out too. He turns to Adel who is flirting with Jenny and the other girls. He walks over to Nora who is sitting by herself in the hot tub looking a bit lost.

Kamil waves to her as he comes closer. She looks up at him and smiles, relieved that she has someone to talk to. Kamil enters cautiously into the hot tub and finds a seat across from her. He enjoys the hot bubbles around him and also the company of his favourite teacher.

"Don't worry about him, Ms. Morgan." He nods towards Adel's direction and smiles at her reassuringly. "He's just playing. He doesn't mean anything by it."

Nora raises her eyebrows and then smiles. "I don't know what you mean, Kamil."

Kamil nods his head, understanding that he should keep his mouth shut. "It was a very great day today. I really am enjoying this retreat."

"Well, I'm very happy to hear this. I am enjoying today too." She can't help but relax when Kamil is around. He had a great way of easing her nerves with his calm and easy-going personality.

"You know, my wife would not have let me come if it weren't for Adel being my chaperone." He chuckles.

"Your wife sure doesn't let you have too much fun, does she?" She says this tongue-in-cheek. She always enjoyed reading Kamil's essays he submitted for writing class. They often described his family life events such as when his wife put him on the couch again because of a comment he made to her about her cooking or some silly thing. When she would call him to read his essay to the class, it often made the class burst out in laughter since he would read with so much expression and humour. Although, he would try to make light of his stories, Nora had a feeling that Kamil was unhappy with his life. She herself didn't understand why he would put up with such immaturity.

He was definitely very intelligent and had a good head on his shoulders. He also knew how to make others laugh and feel good about themselves. This was a trait very rare to find in most people she knew. She genuinely liked Kamil as a person and as a friend. She would hate that he be unhappy in his life. But this of course was not her business so she kept these thoughts to herself.

A new year's resolution, she promised to herself— she will live life to the fullest and not meddle in anyone else's before fixing her own life.

PART THREE

Turkish Drama

Chapter 33

Excuses do not fix things

Nora thinks about the nice conversation she had with Kamil in the hot tub. It made her forget that Adel was having the time of his life showing off his dives while the girls cheered him on. Kamil chatted with her until the pool attendants announced that the pool was closing.   Not only was she relieved to have his company, she really enjoyed their intense discussion about topics ranging from politics to religion.

Now after her shower, sitting on the bed with a towel wrapped around her hair, she relaxes by reading a paperback novel.

There is a soft knock on the door. Nora looks at the time on the clock. It is one a.m. She debates whether she should ignore the knock and pretend she is sleeping. The knocking persists. She gets up and throws on her robe and walks to the door.

"Who is it?" she asks.

"It's me…"

"Me who?" She snaps.

"Me, me… who else could it be?"

Exasperated, she flings open the door ready to poke his eyes out.

Adel is leaning on the door frame, dressed in a white T-shirt and snug blue jeans. His hair is slightly damp and he's carrying a towel.

"What do you want?" she asks.

He looks at her a little shocked. "I told you I would come by, did I not?" The elevator opens a few doors down and an older couple walks out chatting happily.

Nora looks down the hall and then pulls him inside, closing the door behind her.

Adel puts his arms around her. She turns and pulls away. She motions for him to sit on the couch.

"What's wrong, Nora?" Adel asks.

She doesn't know why she is upset. Why did she care that Adel was so full of himself? Why did it matter that she saw the real person he was—a big show off and a flirt? Maybe the anger was more at herself. How in the world could she fall for such a shallow person?

"Nora…why aren't you saying anything?"

She turns around. "Nothing. It's nothing. I'm sorry, it's late and I wasn't expecting guests." She sits down in the arm chair.

Adel, unsure of himself, sits down on the couch.

"I have something to tell you… That I've been trying to tell you for some time." He clears his throat.

Nora asks, "What is it?"

Adel takes a deep breath. "Remember when we first met... when I told you how it is in my culture?"

Nora shakes her head slowly. "No..."

He continues, "Well, in my culture, when a boy and a girl reach a certain age, the parents look for partners for them."

Nora says, "Yes, that's right. An arranged marriage, I remember now. What does that have to do with anything?"

Adel looks down into his hands and then back at Nora. Nora suddenly begins to realize what Adel is trying to say.

"I see... You've been arranged to marry someone in Turkey," she says.

Adel looks away nervously. "No..."

"Okay, then what?"

He turns to her and spits out the words. "My parents arranged for me to marry my cousin."

Nora catches her breath. She whispers, "And sooo..."

Adel continues. "We did get married. A month and a half ago. I have been meaning to tell you this...."

Nora's eyes widen. "Are you trying to tell me that... that you're married? Oh my God."

She stands up, nearly falling out of the chair. She stumbles away from him and tries to stable herself against the desk. Adel stands up and follows her. "Wait, Nora, please listen first. Let me explain."

She shakes her head. "Why? Why are you doing this to me? You've been married all along?"

"My cousin and I," he says, "we didn't want this. She is only doing this to please our family. I only did this to uphold my parents' agreement with her parents and my Grand Uncle."

Nora shakes her head in disbelief. "I still don't understand... Why? Why did you make it seem we had something together? A future? You made me doubt my own life. My fiancé..."

Adel tries to pull her to him. "Because we *do* have something together. A future..."

Nora pulls away, shaking her head. "How can you say that? You're *married*, for crying out loud."

Adel pleads. "I thought I'd never see you again," he says. "I never stopped thinking about you. I never knew that fate would bring us back together."

He begins babbling desperately. "After I got deported, I lost sight of the purpose in my life. I was very depressed and miserable," he says. "When I came to Canada, there was nothing here for me. No future, no opportunities. All my dreams were over. I had been staying with Kamil, his new wife and her parents and working for her father in a fast food restaurant. It was awful so I quit and moved out. Homeless and jobless. Kamil was so worried that he told my parents who asked my Grand Uncle to help. So that is how the arrangement was made, all without my knowledge. My Grand Uncle's granddaughter was arranged to marry me in exchange for a portion of land that belongs to my father. But with that my Grand Uncle also released half of the land belonging to my father for my two brothers to build their homes."

Nora turns slowly and looks up at Adel. "So you see Nora," Adel says, "I had no choice but to accept the arrangement. It was my duty. And I thought that I could try to make the marriage work. I had nothing left to look forward to do. I hadn't seen my cousin since we were kids. She was annoying then. But I thought maybe she has grown up, changed. When we were married, she looked like a traditional Turkish wife. But the minute we got to her apartment, she showed her true colours. She told me right then that she's only doing this to please our family. We both agreed to stay out of each other's way. So you see, we had not fulfilled our marriage commitment."

Nora frowns. "I don't understand."

Adel grabs her hand. "We did not consummate our marriage," he says. "We have been living like brother and sister. I sleep in the guest room. I live my own life. She smokes, drinks, takes drugs... all the things I detest. She swears... she is rude and loud. She also has a boyfriend she talks on the phone with late at night. I'm guessing this is the reason why she was arranged to marry me... so that Grand Uncle and his daughter (my aunt) would not be shamed by her behaviour. Kamil told me after we were married that Yonka had been sent here to Canada because of some scandal back home."

Does he think I'm a moron? Nora is completely stunned. "This still does not change the fact that you are a married man, Adel."

Adel lowers his voice, again reaching for her hand. "Don't you see? When you walked into the classroom that day after thinking I would never see you again... I was brought back to life," he says. "I was re-born. It was then and there that I decided that I would annul my arranged marriage. I would end the farce and face my family. "

Nora whirls around. "Why would you do that? You know that I'm engaged to be married," she says. "What makes you think that I would give that all up for you?"

Adel grabs her arm and pulls her to him. "Because I know you feel the same as I do. Because I see you in my life forever. Because I'm so in love with you, I can't think straight when you are not close to me..."

Nora closes her eyes. She tenses up. "I don't know why I am doing this...This is crazy... This is..."

Adel whispers, "Tell me to go... If this isn't what you want. Tell me to go..." She stares at him unable to respond. They stand in silence for what seems like hours.

He nods his head, finally accepting that this was not going any further. He turns around and with tired steps, he walks to the door. He looks back but Nora has turned away from him. He sees her silhouette—a goddess frozen in ice. He opens the door and leaves.

.

Chapter 34

What's life without drama?

Yonka has been very busy. She just spent the last hour turning over picture frames, flower vases, and knick knacks in her living room. She pushed chairs onto their sides, and took paintings off the walls. She was careful not to destroy anything since she purchased these things with her own hard earned money. Earlier she had been in Adel's room searching for his little black phone book. She rummaged through his dresser, his suitcase and read through all his papers. When she found what she was looking for, she tossed all his belongings on the floor, not caring if anything got broken. All his things were junk, for all she cared. He was such a neat freak, always complaining about her leaving her nail polish on the coffee table or dirty plates on the counter. He would have a fit when he saw all his precious belongings thrown on the floor.

It was exhausting but liberating. She checks herself out in the mirror over the fire place mantle. She sees her hazel green eyes stare right back at her. Her dark wavy hair frames her face. Her cheeks are slightly pink from all the running around. I look quite sexy when I'm flushed with excitement, she thinks to herself. She smiles at her reflection for a second more and then remembers that she has a mission to accomplish.

She picks up the phone and dials 9-1-1, the local emergency phone number.

When the call is answered, she blurts into the phone. "I need help! Someone broke into my home!"

"9-1-1. What's the address of the emergency?"

She sobs. "5988 Forest Pine, Suite 309, Vancouver."

"Who am I speaking with?" the 911 attendant asks.

"Yonka... Yonka Emre. E-M-R-E." She throws in a couple of more sobs.

"Now tell me what the exact problem is."

"Like I said, I need help! Someone broke into my home!" She starts to sob uncontrollably.

"Okay, please calm down. We're sending a patrol car over right away. We will call you at this number if we need to contact you."

Yonka smiles to herself as she hangs up the phone.

***

Kamil had gone straight to bed after coming back from the pool. Ayca had called to check on him. He told her that he was tired and needed to rest. She continued yattering away. She told him that next time she would not let him go on these *official school activities.* Finally, after assuring her that he had been a good boy, she hung up the phone.

He had just dozed off into a deep sleep thinking of the lovely evening he had with Ms. Morgan when he

is startled awake by the ringing of his cell phone—
actually, it was the ring tone of Justin Timberlake's
"Cry Me a River" (which, if you asked Adel, was silly
for a grown man to have on his phone). Adel, on the
other hand, had Eminem's "Lose Yourself" as his
ringtone because he was in fact, the Turkish Slim
Shady.

So let's go back to Kamil who was rudely
awakened by Justin Timberlake singing "But I refuse,
you must have me confused with some other guy...Cry
me a river...." He drowsily reaches for his cell phone.

"Hello..." Kamil mumbles.

"I need to talk to Adel," Yonka sobs into the
phone. "I have been trying to call him all evening but
he is not answering his cell!"

"What's wrong? What's the matter?" Kamil asks,
"Is everything okay?"

Yonka says, "I came home from work and found
the place had been robbed."

Kamil sits up. "What?! Are you okay? Did you call
the police?"

Yonka starts crying. "Yes, I did... I was so
scared." She was at Guy's apartment sitting at his

kitchen table. Guy was reading his magazine across from her, smirking at Yonka's colourful performance of a damsel in distress.

Kamil asks, "Where are you now?"

"I'm at my friend's place for the night. I want to talk to my husband."

"Okay," Kamil says. "Wait a minute."

He climbs out of his bed, the chill wrapping its fingers around his bare back. He walks down the hall to Adel's room. He knocks softly on the door. There is no response. Kamil opens the door and sees that the bed has not been slept in. He shakes his head, knowing full well of Adel's playboy ways. He had to cover for him many a time back in the old days when Adel would have two or three girlfriends at once. Kamil goes back to the room. He picks up his cell phone which he had left on the bed.

"Yonka…"

"What took you so long?" Yonka barks.

Kamil rolls his eyes. "Adel is probably asleep. He was not very happy today. Very bothered. He kept saying that he is not feeling well."

"Well, wake him up!"

Kamil is beginning to lose his patience. "I'll tell him in the morning. Right now, he's locked himself in the room."

Yonka is livid. "Knock louder! This is important. This is an emergency. Break the door down if you have to."

Guy raises his eyebrows and gives Yonka a *you're being very naughty* look. Yonka shrugs her shoulders and gives him a sly smile.

Kamil raises his voice, losing any ounce of empathy for this woman. "Yonka, as long as you are in a safe place, everything will be fine. Adel is very upset and perhaps, you are the cause of this. I will tell him to call you in the morning."

Yonka is baffled by Kamil's response. "Kamil, I demand you to wake Adel up. Is he there? Or is he somewhere else? Are you protecting him? Is that what this is?!"

Kamil says gruffly, "Yonka... I am offended by your accusations. I'm very tired. Good night." He ends the call and stares into the darkness. After a few seconds, he dials Adel's number. The phone call goes straight to Adel's voice mail.

Kamil leaves a message. "Adel, Yonka called. She is trying to contact you because someone broke into your apartment tonight. Call me back when you get this."

Chapter 35

What a mess this has become

Not only was this trip the worst time of his life, he didn't get any action with Nora when he had the chance to. He had never been turned down by a woman before. Walking back to the hotel suite, Adel checks his voice mail messages. He has five messages—the first message, Yonka asks him to call her back. The second message is Yonka's angry voice asking him why he doesn't answer his phone. The third call—she is furious, threatening that if he doesn't answer his phone or call her back, something bad was going to happen. The next call she is crying hysterically. Then he hears Kamil's message. He quietly enters his suite so as not to wake Zeid who is sleeping on the couch. He walks past him and stumbles over the pile of clothes left on the floor. He mumbles obscenities under his breath as he walks to his room. He opens the door and is startled to see Kamil sitting on his bed.

"Where were you?" Kamil asks. Adel rolls his eyes and drops his towel on the chair.

Kamil says, "Don't worry, I can only guess....Did you get my phone message?"

Adel nods his head. "Yes, I did." He sits on the edge of the bed.

"And..." Kamil says.

Adel frowns. "I don't believe it. Yonka thinks she can continue this crazy plan to keep me from annulling the marriage. She is so wrong."

Kamil is not so sure. "You think this is a trick? Why would she do this? She sounded really upset when I spoke to her."

Adel punches his fist into his hand. "It's just a coincidence that she gave me drugs to try to trick me to believe that we sleep together? I know it is all a trick. Now because I do not answer her phone calls, she thinks up this story so that she can get me to feel sorry for her."

Kamil nods his head slowly. "It does sound strange... Anyway, she said she is at her friend's house until you come home. She demanded to talk to you. When I found out you weren't here, I told her that you were angry and upset and have locked yourself in the room. She didn't believe me. She accused me of covering for you because you were with another woman."

Adel laughs out loud. "See what I mean... she is so afraid of being robbed but she is still thinking about who I am sleeping with? Scared, my ass."

Kamil replies, "I did have that feeling when she first sounded scared and then she was angry demanding me to break down your door."

Adel shakes his head. "Tonight when we get back home, I'm going to phone my father. I am going to ask him to find someone to annul the marriage."

"Yes, it seems best since this is going out of hand," Kamil says. Adel nods his head in agreement.

Kamil gets up and goes back to his room. Part of him hopes that he was not covering for Adel because he had been with Ms. Morgan. He dismisses the thought from his mind as he tries to fall back asleep in his bed.

Adel lies face down on his bed and covers the pillow on his head. He wished that he had never agreed to this arranged marriage thing in the first place. He would have had Nora tonight if he and Yonka were not married.

Chapter 36

Reality is unavoidable

The next afternoon, Kamil accompanies Adel to Yonka's apartment. Adel wanted to make sure that he had a witness. Knowing Yonka, it was possible anything could happen. When they enter the apartment, they are greeted by the mess that Yonka left for the police to mark as evidence of the burglary.

Adel enters his bedroom. He sees his belongings strewn all over the floor and starts cursing the day he agreed to marry his crazy cousin.

Kamil walks into the room. Adel's dresser had been emptied and his clothes looked like they had been trampled on by stiletto heeled boots.

Kamil sighs. "So you think Yonka would do something like this?"

Adel waves his arms in the air. "Yeah, I do think so. If she can drug me and try to make me believe that we sleep together, yes, she can do just about anything to get her way."

Kamil shakes his head. "But what does she get out of this? If she has her own life, why would she want to stay with this "fake" marriage?"

Adel can't figure it out either. "Maybe she just wants to have Grand Uncle leave her alone. Who knows?"

***

Adel asks Kamil to help him clean up his room. Over the years, Kamil has put up with Adel's weird obsession for keeping everything neat. After putting everything back in order, Adel decides to call his father. He asks Kamil for a long distance calling card.

Kamil gives him one. Why Adel never buys one for himself, he will never know. Adel dials his home phone number in Istanbul.

His father answers the phone in his rough usual manner. "Alo?"

Adel's father had not heard from Adel in months hoping and praying that he and Yonka were getting along.

"Father, I am calling to ask for you to arrange for the sheikh to annul my marriage to Yonka."

Adel's father cannot believe his ears. "Why do you want to shame your family? How can you request such a thing?"

Adel is insistent. "Father, Yonka and I will never be like husband and wife. She lives her own life. She drinks, she smokes, she takes drugs."

Adel's father shakes his head, still in shock. He stands up from the couch while Adel's mother holds him steady. What was going on? What is Adel saying to him?

Adel's father cries out. "Why do you say things about your wife?"

Sammy runs into the room to see what the commotion is. He goes to his father's side, worried that something might happen.

Adel replies angrily, "Because it is the truth. She told me right after the marriage ceremony to let her live her life and I live my own. We sleep in separate rooms and do everything separately like roommates."

Kamil sits quietly, trying to support his friend by giving him reassuring looks.

Adel's father cries out. "It is your responsibility to try to be a husband to her."

Adel can't take it anymore. If his father wasn't going to listen, he will just have to tell him bluntly.

He bursts out. "She has a lover who she talks to on the phone every night. I don't care about that because I already decided that I do not want to continue with this farce of a marriage."

Adel's father is so furious that he ignores the sharp pain in his left arm. He yells into the phone, "Adel, this is going to destroy your mother. It is going to..." He stops.

"I'm sorry but I cannot live like this," Adel says. "I want to stop this before it goes too far. I am still young. I want to have a real marriage and have children. I thought I could go through with this to 'do the right thing' but I didn't realize that it would be with someone who is only trying to hide from the family her 'real' life. Father, I..."

"Stop!" Adel's father gasps. He clutches his chest. Adel's mother screams and puts her arms around her husband as he falls onto the couch. Adel's sisters start screaming when they see their father's face crumpled in pain.

Adel cries into the phone, "Father, Father! What is happening?!"

Sammy picks up the phone. "Adel, Father is having chest pain. We are going to bring him to the hospital. I'll call you later." The line goes dead.

Adel stares at the phone. Kamil looks at him unsure of what happened. Adel begins pounding his fist into his hand. Tears are streaming from his face.

"What happened?" Kamil asks. "Adel, tell me what happened?"

Adel weeps uncontrollably and buries his face into his hands.

Chapter 37

Hurricane Yonka

Nora decided that she had to confess everything to Michael. She meets him at a café hoping that being in a public place Michael wouldn't be able to pull his "I'm listening, but not really" stunt on her again. She calmly explains to him that she had been seeing Adel over the last few weeks but that nothing had come out of it, except for a couple of kisses. She half expected Michael to rationalize the situation and tell her that now that this was out of her system, they could go get married and live happily ever after.

Michael slams his napkin on the table.

"So that's it? All the years we've been together and you gave it all up? For what? Your student?"

Nora fumbles for a reasonable explanation but finds none. "I told you. He wasn't a student when we met."

Michael gets up and puts his jacket on.

He says loudly, "Whatever! You know you've really lost it, Nora. I really don't know what to say to you anymore."

Nora is silent. Knowing that there was no turning back now, she takes the engagement ring off her finger and slides it across the table to Michael. He looks at her with disgust, grabs the ring and says under his breath, "Have a nice life."

He turns around and pushes himself through the crowd and leaves her sitting there in complete shock.

***

Kamil helps Adel pack his suitcase. "I should go with you. Your family is like family to me."

Adel turns to look at him speechless. Kamil gives him a hug. He has never seen Adel so upset before.

***

At Guy's apartment, Yonka has Adel's sports bag open with his personal contents spread out on the table. In her hand is Nora's business card. She turns it over and sees scribbled on the back is Nora's cell phone number. She dials the number.

***

Humiliated by the events in the café, Nora sits in her car getting ready to drive home. As she turns the key in the ignition, her cell phone rings. She looks at the number but doesn't recognize it. She answers cautiously, "Hello?"

"Hello, is this Nora?"

Nora says, "Yes, who is this?"

"I'm Adel's sister. He speaks of you all the time."

Nora pauses. "Sister? I didn't know his sister was in town."

"He doesn't tell you much, does he? But he speaks of you very much."

Who was this weird woman calling her cell phone? Nora begins to panic. "Why are you calling me?"

"Were you with Adel last night? We were trying to call him but he did not answer his phone. You see it was an emergency, his apartment had been broken into..."

Nora can't believe what she is hearing. "Is this some sick joke? Who the hell is this?"

Yonka pauses and then says seriously, "I am Adel's wife. I want to know, were you with him last night?"

Nora although shocked, says calmly, "You should talk to Adel."

Yonka growls, "Leave my husband alone. Do you hear me?"

Nora repeats even more calmly, "I think you better talk to him."

Yonka is surprised with this woman's calmness. "Do you have something to hide? Do you go after married men to screw their lives?! Or are they better in bed?"

Nora did not appreciate being accused of something she did not do. She didn't know Yonka at all but found her to be a completely annoying bitch.

She replies, "He told me the whole situation between both of you. He said he is going to annul the marriage."

Yonka goes ballistic. "Do you realize what you've done? You whore!"

This woman was simply incredible! Nora says, "That's enough. Don't call me again!"

Yonka screams into the phone, "I'm pregnant! He wants to leave me for you, a home wrecking slut!"

Nora knew that Adel was a player but this news took her completely off guard. "I don't believe you! He said that both of you haven't even slept together. That's why he is going to get an annulment."

"Of course he'd say that to you," Yonka says. "He wanted to get into your pants. And you fell for it. Did he tell you that I'm pregnant? And that's the reason why he wants to end our marriage?"

"I don't believe you," Nora says.

Yonka knows she hit a nerve. "You believe him because he told you that we are like brother and sister?" she asks.

Oh my goodness, I can't believe I'm having this conversation, Nora thinks to herself.

"This is absolutely ridiculous. Leave me alone. Stop calling me." Nora ends the call.

She starts her car, prepared now to go straight home and pour herself a glass of red wine and try to forget all this craziness she let herself get into. Before she pulls out into traffic, her cell phone beeps. She looks down at it. There is a new text message. Out of curiosity, she puts her car into park and checks the message.

Her phone says "receiving three image files." As the files download, she sees the first photo— Yonka and Adel in an intimate kiss in their bed. The second photo—Adel's face pressed against Yonka's bosom. And finally, the last photo—Adel and Yonka cuddling, and Yonka smiling at the camera. Nora shuts the engine and sits dumbfounded. She could not believe how she had been duped by Adel's charm and good looks. She lost her fiancé because of this good-for-nothing creep!

She punches the steering wheel and begins to cry.

Chapter 38

Father and son

Adel's suitcase is packed. Kamil was looking online at travel websites to see the cost of the next flight to Istanbul when Adel's cell phone rings.

It is Adel's mother and she tells him that they are at the hospital and that his father is fine.

She says, "Thank God, it was only a small attack. The doctors were able to make him better right away."

Adel waves to Kamil to stop searching online. He is so relieved to hear the news. "Oh Ma, thank God. Thank God. I'm so sorry."

His mother's reassuring voice eases his nerves. "Do not be sorry. It is not your fault. Your father wants to speak with you." She hands the phone to her husband. Adel can hear some whispering and then finally his father speaks into the phone.

"Adel..."

Adel interrupts. "I'm sorry, Father. I did not want to get you sick over this. I'm coming home on the next airplane to Istanbul."

"Stop. Let me speak." His father clears his throat.

Adel nods his head. "Yes, Father."

"Maybe it is good this thing happened. It gave me time to think about my life. You know you are right...right about me being weak."

Adel moans, "Nooo, you are not weak..."

His father continues. "Let me finish. I thought I could keep the peace. I owe a lot to your Grand Uncle," he says. "You know he was like a father to me when your grandfather died. But I think I was too blind to see. To see what Grand Uncle has done to oppress me and my family. I should have not agreed to this marriage between you and Yonka. It is known here about Yonka's ways. There were stories about how she was here before she was sent to Canada. We also heard about how angry her family and Grand Uncle are about some of the things she does in Canada. And yet when your Grand Uncle came to me, I gave in to his request. He convinced me that she was better and that it would be best for both of you to be together. I had my doubts but ... I realize now, it was my weakness that made me give in. Your mother was against this. She is a very wise woman."

Adel's mother rubs her husband's arm lovingly. He looks up at her knowing his life would be so empty without her by his side.

"I know now that you deserve a good woman like your mother. And nothing less."

"Oh, Father..." Adel never heard him say such adoring things about his mother.

Adel's father smiles. "I have already contacted the sheikh. The annulment is now in process."

Adel is shocked. "Father, thank you. Thank you..." He could not believe his ears.

"My son. I am so proud of you. You are doing what I always dreamed of doing. I wanted to see the world. Doesn't mean I regret my life. I am grateful to

God for your mother and your brothers and sisters. You all are my treasure. More than any money or land could give to me..."

Adel nods his head still in disbelief.

His father's voice trails and begins to cough. He hands the phone to his wife.

Adel's mother says to Adel, "Your father must rest now. Call us again tomorrow? I love you, my son."

Adel never felt so close to his family as he did in this moment.

"I love you too, Ma."

Chapter 39

Confrontations

Adel and Kamil are ready to leave the apartment. Adel has all his belongings in the hallway when Yonka enters. The three of them stand awkwardly in the foyer.

Yonka blurts out, "What's going on?"

Kamil looks away.

Adel turns and walks down the hallway. "I'm leaving."

Yonka frowns and follows him. "What? Do you think you're going to get away so easy?"

Adel does not look her in the eye. "Look, you know already that I want to annul the marriage. I was going to move out at the end of the month. But it is best if I do it now." He nods to Kamil and they start walking towards the door. Yonka grabs Adel's arm. He turns and looks at her surprised.

"I won't let you," Yonka says.

"Won't let me what?" He looks at her in disbelief.

"My grandfather won't let this happen," she says. "You can't leave."

Adel nods his head and gives her a sarcastic smile. "Oh yeah? My parents have already arranged the annulment," he says. "There is nothing you or Grand Uncle can do to stop it." He pulls his arm from her in disgust. "Come on, Kamil, let's go."

Yonka snaps. "I hope that little hussy was worth it."

Adel turns to her. "What did you say?"

"Yeah, I know you slept with that whore," she says. "That's what all this is about."

Adel raises his hand and then he pulls his arm back ready to give her a good slap. Kamil shakes his head and gives him a disapproving look.

Adel lowers his voice. "You are such a bitch. Stay away from me."

He motions to Kamil. "Come on, Kamil. Let's go." They both walk out the door.

"You donkey!" Yonka yells. "You won't get away with this!" How did her plans turn into such a mess?

The ringing of her phone startles her. Yonka walks to the living room and answers it.

"Hello?"

"Granddaughter," her grandfather says. "Why is Adel going to annul the marriage?"

Yonka stops for a moment. "Hello Grandfather." She starts to cry. She whimpers, "He is seeing a woman."

Her grandfather is shaking with anger. "What? You have proof of this?"

Yonka nods. "Yes, I spoke to the other woman." She whimpers into the phone.

"Okay... stop crying. He tells his parents, your aunt and uncle, that you both live like brother and sister. That the marriage was not ..."

"That's a lie!" she exclaims. "How can he say this about his wife?"

"Can you prove he is lying?"

"Yes, I have pictures of the two of us on our honeymoon—of us together, romantic," she says.

Her grandfather pauses. "Okay... that's good but may not be enough. His parents, your aunt and uncle, believe him."

Yonka takes a deep breath. "I am pregnant," she says softly.

Her grandfather's eyes widen. "That is all the proof I need," he says. "Congratulations, my granddaughter."

She cries harder—partly because she is upset and scared that the truth will come out.

"Shh... shhh.. Granddaughter. Don't worry. Grandfather will take care of all of this. You just take care of yourself. I will call again."

Yonka hangs up the phone. She is numb, unsure of what the future will hold for her and her baby.

Chapter 40

Is love really only an illusion?

Adel and Kamil are driving in Adel's car. Kamil says, "Stay with us until you find your own place."

Adel shakes his head. "Thank you, but I don't want to impose on you and your family."

"You won't be imposing on me," Kamil insists.

Adel says, "Okay, what I mean is I don't want to impose on your wife and *her* family."

Kamil chuckles to himself. He couldn't argue with that.

"Seriously, I'll be fine," Adel says. "If I need anything, I'll call you." He arrives at Kamil's building.

Kamil opens the door and steps out. He turns back and leans into the window.

Kamil asks, "So what are you going to do now?"

Adel shakes his head. "Not sure yet. But I'll be okay," he says.

* * *

Adel looks up Nora's address on his smart phone. He drives to her townhouse in a suburb which is forty-five minutes away from the city. It takes him some time to find her address but he is very good at reading Google maps from his experience as a shuttle driver. When he arrives at the townhouse complex, he parks his car in the visitor parking. He dials Nora's number on his cell phone.

* * *

Nora is sitting on her bed. She had just finished talking with Kamil—telling him everything that happened at Whistler, Yonka's phone call and her break-up with Michael. She must have sounded hysterical but Kamil's patience and kind words helped her calm her nerves. She was ready to go to sleep when her cell phone rings. She checks the caller ID and sees that it is Adel. Why is he calling me now? She hesitates a moment before she answers her phone.

"Hello Nora?"

Nora pauses. Finally she says, "Hi Adel."

There is an awkward silence.

Adel says, "I miss you. Can I come see you?"

Nora shakes her head. "I am a bit tired. Can we do this tomorrow?"

"Is everything all right, Nora?"

Nora says quietly, "Not really. I've got a lot on my mind right now."

"I see..."

Nora does not know what to say next.

Adel nods his head. "Well, I won't keep you."

She bites her lip. "Adel..."

"I am sorry for bothering you." Adel is about to end the call.

"Wait. You're right. I think we do need to talk. Can you come by my place?"

"I don't know what's going on... I had some good news to tell you but it seems you are cold to me now."

Nora continues. "I'm sorry. It's just that your wife Yonka called me today."

"What?"

Nora is holding back her tears but she can't help it now. Adel says, "I'm right outside. I'm coming up right now."

Nora nods her head and hangs up the phone.

Chapter 41

Istanbul, Turkey

Adel's Grand Uncle is at the home of his parents. It is very rare for him to visit Adel's family home. Adel's mother prepares a plate of sweets and fruit. Juliana serves the coffee to his Grand Uncle and their father. After taking a sip of coffee, Grand Uncle gives Adel's father a look which signals to everyone that the serious talk will now begin. Adel's father waves to the girls to leave the room.

Grand Uncle begins, "Adel must fulfill his marriage commitment."

Adel's father says, "The two are not living as husband and wife. Yonka lives her own life as a single western woman, smoking, drinking, and has a boyfriend."

"Who says these things?" Grand Uncle asks, "You believe your good-for-nothing son? He just wants everything easy life and when it doesn't work out for him, he runs away."

Adel's father is angry but he tries to keep his composure. "Uncle," he says, "I have already approved the annulment. The process is underway. It is best for both Yonka and Adel."

Grand Uncle becomes furious. He waves his arms in the air. "No, I will talk to the sheikh," he says in a loud voice. "This annulment cannot take place. Adel *must* fulfill his obligation or else..."

Adel's father frowns. "Uncle, the decision is mine and not yours to make."

Grand Uncle wags his finger. "Adel has to fulfill his obligation as a husband to his wife AND to his child."

Adel's father starts to speak and then stops. He is confused.

Grand Uncle continues. "Yes, so your son did not tell you the *reason* why he wants to annul the marriage," he says. "He has another woman, and when he finds his wife is pregnant, he wants to run away."

Adel's father says quietly, "Uncle, I do not believe this of my son. If he says, he and Yonka have not consummated the marriage, I believe him. He is a responsible man."

Grand Uncle stands up. "Are you saying my granddaughter is a liar?!"

Adel's father says, "I am saying that I believe my son."

Grand Uncle shakes his finger at Adel's father. "If your son does not honour his commitment as husband to Yonka, you will pay for this."

Adel's father stands up looking eye to eye with his Uncle. He says, "Uncle, everyone knows well of Yonka's ways. I think it will be revealed soon who has honoured or not honoured their marriage commitment."

Grand Uncle raises his hands up in frustration. "Have you gone mad?" Grand Uncle looks up to the sky and yells, "Oh dear God, what have I done to deserve this? I've treated this man like a son and this is how he shows his gratefulness?" He walks past Adel's father and out the door.

* * *

Later that night, Adel's parents are sitting at the kitchen table. Adel's father holds his head in his hands. Adel's mother puts her arm around her husband.

She says, "What are you going to do?"

Adel's father looks up. "We know that even if Adel is not the father of Yonka's child, it would be honourable for him to stay with Yonka."

Adel's mother sighs deeply shaking her head.

He continues. "But should our son suffer because of Yonka's loose ways?"

Adel's mother touches her husband's hand. "We should stand behind our son," she says.

Adel's father nods his head in agreement. He stands up. "Of course we will. No matter what the consequences."

* * *

At that same moment, Adel's Grand Uncle is in his office, on the phone still waving his arms around—furious with Adel's father's defiance.

He yells into the phone, "Do what you have to. Find him and talk sense into him!" He pauses. "I said whatever you have to do. If he doesn't cooperate, bring him home."

Chapter 42

Adel and Nora

Adel climbs up the steps to Nora's porch and rings the doorbell. He is livid that Yonka would have the nerve to call her.

Meanwhile, Nora is in the bathroom, splashing water on her face. She dries her eyes and stares at herself in the mirror. Adel rings the doorbell again.

Nora takes a deep breath and then goes down the stairs—each step seems surreal, as if she is floating. The last few days of events seem like a crazy dream. Her life was so straight forward before she met Adel.

She finally finds herself at the front door. She can see Adel's shape in the frosted glass slats. She opens the door and walks back to the centre of the foyer. She looks pensively ahead, her back to the door. Adel comes inside the house cautiously. He looks at her unsure of what to say.

"Nora, say something."

Nora turns to Adel, her eyes wide with tears. She says, "I didn't realize how complicated this was going to be..."

Adel interrupts her. "What are you talking about?"

Nora says, "You and I. It seems that everything is against us being together."

Adel reaches out to hold her hand. She pulls away.

Adel says, "I can't believe that Yonka would stoop so low to call you. I don't know what she said to upset you, but I can only imagine. She would say or do anything to get her way."

Nora whirls around angrily. "She's your wife! Why wouldn't she be upset that her husband is with another woman? And I can't believe that I am the other woman! Never in my life would I imagine that I would be the home wrecker."

She starts to cry. Adel reaches out and hugs her. She tries to pull away but then puts her head on his shoulder—too exhausted to fight. Adel strokes her hair and holds her tight. Adel speaks softly, "You're not the other woman. You are the only woman for me. I'm only married on paper. I spoke to my father and he will start the annulment immediately. Yonka has always been spoiled. It's always her way or no way. She doesn't want me to annul the marriage because she wants my Grand Uncle to think that she is a good girl now. She wants to hide behind the marriage so that my Grand Uncle will leave her alone and just send her the money."

The sound of Adel's voice is soothing, almost hypnotic. But suddenly, everything is sharp and clear in Nora's mind.

She pulls away again and says angrily, "I can't believe I'm falling for this again. Do you mean what you say or are you so smooth? You say Yonka will do anything to get her way. But I have a feeling you would say anything to get *your* way."

She starts to climb up the stairs. Adel follows after her, reaching for her arm.

"Nora, why are you saying these things?"

Nora is shaking with emotion but then she pulls away. "I'm sorry, Adel. You need to fix your life first... and I need to figure out about mine."

"Nora..."

"Just leave..." She doesn't look him in the eye.

Adel sees that Nora has made up her mind. He shakes his head as he turns and walks to the door. He doesn't look back as he opens the door and leaves. The door closes softly behind him.

Nora's knees suddenly go weak and she sits down on the step. She buries her face into her hands and cries. This is the right thing to do... but what does the future have in store for her?

Chapter 43

Adel and Kamil

Kamil is in bed and is awakened by his ringing cell phone. He reaches out to answer it.

"Hello?"

"Kamil, I need to see you," Adel says.

"Do you know what time it is?" He glances at the clock. It is one o'clock a.m. in the morning.

"It's important."

"Is everything okay?" Kamil sits up.

Adel shakes his head. "Come outside. I'm parked in the driveway."

Kamil climbs out of bed quietly so as not wake Ayca. He puts on a jacket, a pair of pants and his shoes. He slips out of the apartment and goes down to meet Adel.

When he gets into the car, Adel pulls out of the driveway and speeds down the street.

"So what's going on?" Kamil asks.

Adel slams his hand on the steering wheel. "Nora broke up with me," he says. "Yonka found Nora's number and called her. She told Nora something to make her doubt me. I need to fix this *now*."

Kamil is not surprised. "Why do you want to complicate things?" he asks. "Deal with this mess first with Yonka and then..."

Adel interrupts him. "I have to convince Nora to be my wife."

Kamil can't believe it. "Are you serious? Have you thought about how it would be if you and Nora got married?"

Adel says, "Yes... well... no...it doesn't matter."

"But it *does* matter," Kamil insists. "First of all, does she really know who you are? Would she ever want to live in Istanbul? Would she be satisfied with the fact that you are just starting out. You have no job, no money."

Adel didn't need to hear this from Kamil and he swerves the car.

Kamil cries out, "Hey Adel, slow down!"

Instead of listening, Adel puts his foot on the pedal and speeds up.

Kamil looks nervously at Adel. "Adel... come on.. Stop the car. Let's get some coffee..."

Adel slams on the brakes, pulls the steering wheel sharply to the left and does a U-turn in the street into on-coming traffic.

Kamil raises his voice. "What's going on, Adel?"

Adel says angrily under his breath, "I'll drop you back to your *safe* life, Kamil. You don't need to get mixed up in my mess."

Kamil shuts his mouth for the rest of the ride. This is the thanks I get for trying to help, he thinks to himself.

Adel drives up to his building. Kamil gets out of the car, slams the door and walks back into the apartment without looking back.

Chapter 44

Confession

Outside Yonka's apartment, Mirwan and three men are sitting in a dark van waiting and watching. Through the glass, they see Adel entering the lobby and going into the elevator.

* * *

When Mario called earlier that evening to say that he was back in town, Yonka was thrilled. He arrived soon after bringing her gifts from Dubai. When he arrived, she told him that she was pregnant with his child. The news brought tears of joy to his eyes. He promised her that he would never leave her again. He hugged her so hard she thought her arms would break. He told her to change into her fanciest dress because he was taking her to the most expensive restaurant in town to celebrate. He kissed her and promised to marry her right away.

In the back of her head she kept thinking to herself that Adel had moved out just in time. She made up her mind to put all her energy to making her relationship with Mario succeed. She truly did love him despite the fact that her family would never accept him. She didn't care anymore. She was choosing Mario, the father of her child and the love of her life. Her grandfather or her family will no longer stop her. Knowing this gave her a sense of peace and confidence that her life might have a happy ending after all.

Mario tells her to hurry. Reservations at the restaurant are for eight o'clock p.m. She grabs her purse and meets him at the door. They both walk into the hallway arm in arm. Everything is so perfect.

Suddenly Yonka has a sinking feeling in her stomach. She hugs Mario's arm as they walk up to the elevator. She worries that if she lets go, he may disappear before her eyes. She presses the elevator button.

The doors open. Standing in front of her is Adel.

"What are you doing here?" she cries out in shock.

Mario shakes his head in confusion, turns to Adel, pokes his finger into his chest and says, "Who the hell are you?"

Adel smirks replying coldly, "I'm Yonka's husband. Who the hell are you?"

Mario's eyes widen. "What?" He turns to Yonka. "Yonka, tell me that this isn't true."

She tries to think of something to say but all that comes out of her mouth is, "Mario, please let me explain…"

Mario's face turns red. "I'm out of here!" He turns and pushes Adel to the side and walks into the elevator.

Yonka tries to move Adel out of her way. "Mario, please… don't go!"

Yonka sees Mario looking at her with disappointment in his eyes. The elevator doors close. She turns around and heads for the stairs.

Adel follows her. "Yonka, we need to talk."

"Adel, leave me alone!"

She runs down the first flight. Adel is right behind her.

"I need to know what you told Nora. I need to know."

What an ass! She whirls around, half wanting to spit in his face.

"I'm pregnant!" She yells.

Adel cannot believe his ears. "You're what?!" He grabs her by the elbow. "I guess you played me from the beginning."

Yonka frowns. "I don't know what the hell you're talking about."

Adel continues. "What did you think was going to happen? You thought I was going to believe that I am the father of your child?"

Yonka doesn't look surprised. She says in a sneer, "You think you're so smart."

Adel glowers at her. "I know it must be difficult for you since the real father of your child doesn't want to have anything to do with *you*."

Yonka's eyes widen in shock and her face turns beet red. She opens her mouth but no sound comes out. She tries again to say something but then stops. She puts her hand to her mouth and turns away. Adel watches her body shake. He clears his throat.

Yonka says in a hoarse voice, "Please go..."

Adel realizes that for the first time, he was witnessing Yonka crying real tears. He was so used to seeing her fake the tears that he never thought she could cry real ones.

His voice softens. "So is that why you did all this?"

She turns around angrily with tears streaking her cheeks.

She snarls, "You don't know *anything* about me... You think you're better than me? You think that you know about life? About love? About the world that we live in? You're living in a Turkish soap opera! You think that everything is going to end up happily ever after with that girlfriend of yours?"

Adel snaps, "Don't talk about her!"

"Sure, love is great when it's fresh and new," she says bitterly, "but then reality hits you in the face."

Adel shakes his head. "You don't know anything about love. The only person you've ever loved is yourself."

Yonka puts her face in her hands and weeps.

Adel gives a big sigh and takes a step toward her saying quietly, "I came here wanting to ruin your life the way you ruined mine. But it looks like you beat me to it."

He holds her arm.

Yonka turns sharply, disgusted by his touch. She screams, "Let me go!" She loses her balance.

"Yonka!" Adel cries. He reaches out for her hand but it is too late.

Yonka's foot slips off the step and she falls forward down the flight of stairs. Her scream echoes throughout the stairwell. There is a soft thud sound as her body hits the landing below. Her body is lifeless, crumpled up like a rag doll.

Adel rushes down the stairs and kneels beside her.

Suddenly the doors open and Mario rushes into the stairwell. He had heard Yonka's screams from the lobby.

"Yonka, Yonka!" Mario cries as he sees his true love, the mother of his child, lying on the ground. He kneels beside her and yells her name over and over.

Adel gets up and tells Mario, "I'm going to get help. Call 9-1-1."

Mario quickly takes his cell phone out and dials 9-1-1. Adel runs out into the lobby screaming for help.

Chapter 45

Action

Suddenly, Adel is grabbed by a man in dark clothes and dragged into a black van. Two other men in dark clothes shut the van door. Inside the van Adel struggles as one man ties his arms behind his back. The other man covers his nose and mouth with a cloth, doused in chloroform. Adel passes out.

* * *

Adel wakes up and finds himself tied to a steel chair. His eyes slowly adjust to the dim lighting. Mirwan is standing in front of him with three men behind him. Adel tries to move and realizes he cannot.

Mirwan says, "You really got yourself fucked up this time."

Adel gives Mirwan a dirty look. He struggles.

Mirwan says, "Tsk. Tsk. Tsk. If you think we're here because of what went down between you and me... you're wrong. This is bigger than that."

Adel looks confused. "What the hell are you talking about?"

Mirwan motions for one of the men to come over. The man smacks Adel in the face hard causing his nose to bleed.

Mirwan continues. "Like I said, this is bigger than that. Your Grand Uncle sent us to talk some sense into you."

Adel becomes more upset. Mirwan shows him a stack of legal papers.

"What's this?" Adel asks.

Mirwan smirks. "You are going to sign these documents stating that you are going to stop the annulment," he says.

Adel laughs. "Never. No one can force me to stay married to that witch."

Mirwan nods to the man again. He walks towards them and punches Adel in the stomach.

Mirwan continues. "You are right about that. If you don't sign the document, then you're coming with us on the next flight to Istanbul."

Adel laughs again. "And what if I don't do either?"

Mirwan smiles and nods to another man. This one brings a laptop towards Adel. On the screen is a streaming video of a camera zoomed in on Nora walking through her living room into her kitchen. Adel's eyes widen.

Mirwan says, "Your little mistress is very pretty, isn't she? She's much too good for someone like you."

Adel yells, "Leave her out of this!" He struggles again.

"Well, you have a choice to make," Mirwan says. "Stay here and sign the paper or go back to Istanbul. Anything other than that, then your pretty little girlfriend is going to pay the price. It seems fairly straightforward to me. "

Understanding the consequences, Adel drops his head down as if to surrender.

"Let's get this fool out of here," Mirwan says. The two men untie Adel and lift him to his feet. Mirwan walks out of the room. The two men follow him, dragging Adel with them.

Chapter 46

Return to Istanbul

In Istanbul, Adel is escorted by Mirwan and the bodyguards to his Grand Uncle's office. Mirwan presents Adel to his Grand Uncle like offering an unblemished lamb to the altar.

"Adel, what a lovely surprise. How was your vacation in America?" Grand Uncle asks with a smile.

Adel glares at him but keeps his mouth shut.

Grand Uncle starts to say something when the phone rings.

"Alo?"

"Hello Grandfather." Yonka's voice sounds strange and distant.

"Yes, are you all right?"

* * *

Yonka looks up from her hospital bed. Mario is sitting beside her, holding her hand. She remembers waking up in the hospital a few hours earlier. Mario was staring at her with an anxious expression. The dark circles under his eyes told her that he had not slept. He smiled, seeing that she was awake.

"Yonka, I am here," he said to her in a soothing voice.

At the time, she could not say a word. She felt groggy from all the pain medication in her system. Instinctively, her hand moved to her belly.

Mario reached out to hold her hand. "Don't worry Yonka," he said. "Our baby is fine. You had a bad fall but you and the baby are okay."

Yonka nodded her head. Tears streamed down her cheeks. Mario wiped them away with his hand. She grasped his hand and held it tight to her face. She never felt so close to someone as she did that very moment.

It was then that she decided to tell Mario everything. If he was serious about marrying her, he had a right to know.

* * *

She is no longer afraid of what her grandfather might say. Mario promised to be by her side. He said this without hesitation after she had told him the whole truth about her marriage to Adel.

"I want to proceed with the annulment," Yonka says to her grandfather on the phone.

"What?"

"Adel is not the father of my baby. Mario is the real father and he wants to marry me." She takes a breath. Mario squeezes her hand reassuringly.

She continues. "I can't pretend to be the person you want me to be anymore."

"You lied to me," her grandfather spits out. "You dirty liar. You tricked me! This is monstrous!"

Adel and Mirwan look at each other, unaware of what was happening.

"I'm sorry it had to end this way. Good-bye Grandfather," Yonka says quietly. She hangs up the phone.

* * *

Grand Uncle weeps into his hands. Mirwan and Adel had never seen him cry before.

"What happened, Grand Uncle?" Mirwan asks softly.

Grand Uncle looks up at Adel and then waves his hand.

"Release him," he says quietly.

Mirwan looks at his men and nods his head to release Adel. The man holding Adel releases his grip from his arm. The other men step to the side. Adel is free to go.

* * *

Moments later, Adel walks into his family home. His mother opens her arms and hugs him. Jowdat and Sammy take turns hugging him. Juliana and Keananna jump up and down waiting for their turn to welcome him. Zeinab is last but not least.

"Big brother, hug me too!" she says. Adel bends down to pick her up. He hugs her tight and rains kisses on her soft cheeks. Her black curls tickle his nose.

Finally, his father steps forward. Adel puts Zeinab down. He walks over to his father. They stand silently for a minute, not knowing what to say. His father breaks the silence by putting his arms around him and hugging him tightly.

"My son. My son," he repeats over and over.

"Father," Adel says to him. He can't remember the last time his father hugged him.

They hug each other, both vowing to themselves that they will not forget this moment. They will never allow personal differences come between them again.

Chapter 47

A year later

A small Turkish village. You see a woman dressed in Turkish attire sweeping the walk way. When she stands up and turns around, you see that she is pregnant. She wipes her brow. You see that it is Yonka. She looks miserable. From inside the home walks out a burly Turkish man with one connected bushy eyebrow and a thick moustache that looks like a huge brush over his lip. He motions to Yonka to come inside the house (maybe to make his breakfast). You see her make a face but then she puts on a plastic smile and nods her head and hurries into the home. The burly man (who we realize now is her new husband—obviously another arranged marriage) smiles and rubs his pot belly stomach and smacks Yonka in the butt as she walks by him.

* * *

"Yonka, wake up," Mario whispers in her ear. Yonka opens her eyes. She looks over and Mario's smoky dark eyes are looking right back at her. He gives her the sweetest smile.

"You must have been having a bad dream," he says.

She nods her head and smiles. "Yes, it was a very bad dream."

She looks over to the side of her bed and sees a pink baby bassinet. She reaches inside and picks up her baby girl.

"Oh, Fatma, our precious baby," she whispers.

Mario reaches over and gives Fatma a kiss. They both marvel at their baby's big brown eyes and ruby red lips.

"She looks just like you," Mario says to Yonka. He kisses her cheek.

"She has your eyes," Yonka insists.

Mario pulls Yonka close to him and enjoys the moment with their baby together.

***

Kamil is packing his suitcase. His wife is crying in the living room with her parents. Kamil's phone rings. He answers the call. The expression on his face is grim as he speaks into the phone. Soon, he picks up his bag and walks out of the apartment. He leaves without looking back.

***

In front of Nora's townhouse, there is a For Sale sign with a SOLD sticker on the top corner. She closes the gate and walks to her car. This is the end of a chapter of her life.

***

In Istanbul, Adel and his brothers have spent the last eight months helping their father build their brand new house. Their house is built on their father's share of the land which is beside his Grand Uncles' home. It is a four storey home, one storey for Adel's parents and a storey for each son once they are married. His sisters will stay with his parents until they marry and move out.

The house has everything his mother always dreamed of. She has a modern kitchen with new appliances. She finally owns her first dishwasher. Now she can spend less time at the kitchen sink and more time to watch her favourite soap operas.

Over the weekend, Adel's family move into their new home. On the first evening, his mother and sisters prepare a feast and invite all their family and friends to celebrate. They enjoy eating the meal outside on their garden patio. You could hear their laughter and music all around the neighbourhood as they celebrate. Adel's Grand Uncle sits at the head table with a proud smile on his face. Beside him sits Adel's father who also smiles proudly. Beside Adel is Salha, an attractive Turkish woman who is the daughter of his mother's doctor. She has clear blue eyes and fiery auburn hair.

Adel and Salha were introduced to each other a few months earlier. At first Adel agreed to meet her just to appease his mother. Later that evening, Adel and

Salha were in an animated discussion which lasted for hours. They debated about the future of internet marketing and online business. He learned that she completed her education in Business Management in Istanbul and was working in her father's company. A few months later, Adel and Salha were engaged to be married.

Chapter 48

Epilogue

So how does this story end? Surprisingly enough, ten years later, Adel and Salha are still living in Istanbul in their own suite on the second floor of Adel's parent's home. They have two children, a boy and a girl. The boy looks like his mother and the girl looks like Juliana, Adel's sister. They are spoiled by everyone, but most especially by Adel's mother and father who favour their first grandchildren over the others.

Adel and Salha run a successful online marketing company which they run from a large office in Istanbul.

Adel's brothers are also married now with their own children, living in their own suites above his.

Juliana is newly married and living just a few minutes away. She and her husband visit her family every week. Keananna is engaged to marry her sweetheart. She still has to finish her studies so they will not marry for another year. It seems like a "Happily Ever After" ending for the Emre family and an end to the story.

So what happened to Kamil, you may be asking yourself. Actually, it may surprise or even shock you with what I have to say next.

This story was told to you by me—Kamil Ilgaz.

I wrote the story trying to approach it with an unbiased view of Adel's life and, with the help of my wife, I believe I succeeded.

Let's rewind back ten years to put everything into context.

***

Ten years ago, I could no longer stand Ayca's control over my life. She was constantly questioning my every move. When it became apparent that our relationship was going nowhere, I told her that I wanted to separate from her. When she absorbed the news, she became hysterical and picked up a knife from the kitchen counter and stabbed me in the stomach. I recall hearing her screams as I collapsed to the floor and passed out. Her father rushed me to the hospital where after a few weeks, I finally recovered.

When I was discharged from the hospital, I packed my suitcase and walked out of Ayca and her family's life forever.

Not having any family and no reason to stay in Canada, I went back to Istanbul.

I watched Adel become much closer to his father and his family. I encouraged him when he told me that he wanted to marry Salha. I was very happy for his fortunes knowing deep down inside that our friendship was changing or already had changed. We saw each other less every day, until finally it was only on special occasions.

I should mention that when I was recovering in the hospital in Vancouver, Nora came to visit me every day. She read to me books, brought me baked goodies and tried to keep my spirits up. When I told her that I was planning to divorce Ayca and move to Istanbul, she told me that it seemed to be the best decision. We promised to keep in touch and did email each other once in a while. But then she started travelling and we too stopped communicating.

The story leads us to a few years after I had moved back to Istanbul. I was finishing my Masters' degree in English Literature at the university. I had heard that a foreign woman was appointed dean of the English department. The fact that a woman landed the position and was a foreigner made it a very hot topic of conversation on campus.

For me, I did not socialize much so I ignored all the gossip. After classes, I would go home to bury myself into reading novels since I had a strong desire to write one myself eventually.

One day, while I was writing the first chapter of my book, my mother came to my room to tell me that I had an important visitor. I remember scratching my head trying to figure out who the "visitor" would be. My mother wouldn't announce any of my friends as "an important visitor" so I was sure it wasn't Adel or his brothers.

As I followed my mother to the salon, a room where we entertain only our most special guests, I saw the silhouette of a woman (her back to me) looking out of the window. Her raven black hair was straight and fell just below her shoulders. She was dressed in a form fitting navy blue jacket and matching skirt which flowed just below her knees. She turned to me as I entered the room and I remember how her green eyes sparkled and her pink rose petal lips opened up to flash me her familiar smile.

"Nora," I heard myself whisper.

"Kamil," she half whispered back.

My mother was smiling from ear to ear and I am sure she wanted to hear the whole conversation but she politely excused herself from the room to get some coffee, leaving the both of us alone.

Nora without hesitation walked towards me with her arms outstretched. I opened my arms too and we hugged. Her perfume tickled my nose as I buried my face into her hair.

It brought back the moment when I last saw her, when we hugged each other good-bye. I was so sure we would never see each other again.

"Kamil, you can let go of me now," Nora said in a teasing tone.

I blushed profusely, and motioned for her to sit on the couch. I sat on a chair across from her.

"What brings you here to Istanbul?" I asked.

Nora smiled and said, "I accepted a position at the university. I start my new job next week."

My mouth dropped. I realized then that Nora was the "foreigner woman" who received the dean's position in the English department. This was fantastic news.

"Congratulations, Nora! The news is all over campus that a foreign woman was going to be the new dean. I am so happy that you got the job."

Nora nodded her head. Not the reaction I was expecting.

"Kamil." She paused. I noticed that her hands were fidgeting with the hem of her jacket. She looked nervous as if she had something more she wanted to say.

At that moment, my heart sank. I imagined then that Nora was going to tell me that she was here to find Adel. The thought made me sick and I didn't know if I could take it. I quickly stood up.

"Nora, I am not sure if you have something else in mind to share with me. But to be honest with you, I don't know if I can hear what you have to say. I've been let down enough in my life. I don't think I can take anymore."

Nora rose quickly and walked towards me. She put her hand on my arm.

"Kamil, I don't know what to say."

I nodded my head, knowing what was coming next.

"Kamil, look at me."

I looked into her eyes, green as the ocean and just as deep. I nodded my head for her to continue.

"I have never stopped thinking about our conversations together. When I was travelling around the world, I felt you were right beside me."

My eyes widened, unsure of what I was hearing was true.

"After I finished my trip in Australia, I realized that I missed the friendship we had.... The friendship we have. I started applying for positions in Istanbul, in hopes that I could move here to be closer to you."

Tears started to silently stream down my face. I was shaking, so overwhelmed by her words.

"Kamil…" she said but before she could finish, I pulled her close to me and kissed her like I always dreamed of doing since the first day I saw her standing in front of the classroom.

And so what else can I say? Nora and I married each other a year later. We are happily together now with two wonderful sons. We live in Canada where Nora is the director of the English as a Second Language School at the university and I am an English literature instructor. She is the one who encouraged me to finish this novel. She helped me with the editing and filling in the parts that needed a woman's touch.

And so finally, I dedicate this novel to Adel. Although we have drifted apart over the years, I will never forget the times we shared.

But more importantly, I also dedicate this novel to Nora who is my soul mate, my lover, the mother of my sons and my best and truest friend. Thank you Nora for the love and support you give to me. At last I can share this story and close this chapter of our lives.

Kamil Ilgaz, August 2012

Dear Reader,

I want to thank you for reading *Almost a Turkish Soap Opera*. I was so fortunate to have the story adapted into a feature film and web series, which was my directorial debut. See the characters come to life by visiting the official website at www.almostaturkishsoapopera.com.

If you enjoyed this book, please take a few minutes to submit a review on Amazon and on GoodReads. Your kind support will help other readers like you find my books.

For more information about my other books and film projects, visit my blog at http://www.anne-raevasquez.com or send me a tweet @write2film.

Till our paths cross again,

Anne-Rae Vasquez

Before you go

Please check out my latest novels and as a thank you, I'm giving away a free novel if you sign up to my book club. I give away a lot of books from other authors and gift cards so I encourage you to join. Visit Amongus.ca to get your copy.

About the Author

Anne-Rae Vasquez's latest novels, *RESIST, book 2 of the Among Us Trilogy* and *Imminent*-a Truth Seeker Conspiracy Thriller were released in November 2014. REVEAL, book 3 is set to be released in the Fall of 2015. *Doubt*, Book 1 of the Among Us Trilogy was a Gold winner in the Readers' Favorite Book Awards 2014. Doubt was launched at the Raindance Book Festival in 2013.

Her previous novel Almost a Turkish Soap Opera was adapted into a screenplay and later produced into an award winning feature film and web series and was her directorial debut. Her other works include: Gathering Dust - a collection of poems, Salha's Secrets to Middle Eastern Cooking Cookbook published by AR Publishing Inc. and Teach Yourself Great Web Design in a Week, published by Sams.net (a division of Macmillan Publishing).

In her parallel life, she hosts/produces Fiction Frenzy TV, a weekly VLog channel featuring indie artists, authors, filmmakers and musicians. In addition to this, she freelances as a journalist for Digital Journal and manages a design production department.

See you on my blog at www.anne-raevasquez.com .